P9-BZJ-258

HENRY REED'S
THINK TANK

OTHER YEARLING BOOKS YOU WILL ENJOY:

HENRY REED, INC., *Keith Robertson*
HENRY REED'S BABY-SITTING SERVICE, *Keith Robertson*
HENRY REED'S BIG SHOW, *Keith Robertson*
HENRY REED'S JOURNEY, *Keith Robertson*
HOW TO EAT FRIED WORMS, *Thomas Rockwell*
THE GREAT BRAIN, *John D. Fitzgerald*
THE GREAT BRAIN REFORMS, *John D. Fitzgerald*
THE GREAT BRAIN DOES IT AGAIN, *John D. Fitzgerald*
ME AND MY LITTLE BRAIN, *John D. Fitzgerald*

YEARLING BOOKS/YOUNG YEARLINGS/YEARLING CLASSICS are designed especially to entertain and enlighten young people. Charles F. Reasoner, Professor Emeritus of Children's Literature and Reading, New York University, is consultant to this series.

For a complete listing of all Yearling titles,
write to Dell Readers Service,
P.O. Box 1045, South Holland, Illinois 60473.

HENRY REED'S THINK TANK

By Keith Robertson

A YEARLING BOOK

Published by
Dell Publishing
a division of
The Bantam Doubleday Dell Publishing Group, Inc.
666 Fifth Avenue
New York, New York 10103

Copyright © Keith Robertson, 1986

All rights reserved. No part of this book may be reproduced or transmitted in any form or by any means, electronic or mechanical, including photocopying, recording, or by any information storage and retrieval system, without the written permission of the Publisher, except where permitted by law. For information address: Viking Penguin Inc., New York, New York 10010.

The trademark Yearling® is registered in the U.S. Patent and Trademark Office.

ISBN: 0-440-40104-6

This edition published by arrangement with Viking Penguin Inc.

Printed in the United States of America

November 1988

10 9 8 7 6 5 4 3 2 1

CW

HENRY REED'S THINK TANK

Sunday, August 18

My name is Henry Harris Reed and this is my private journal. I am staying with my aunt and uncle in Grover's Corner, New Jersey. Grover's Corner isn't a real town, just a cluster of ten houses near Princeton, New Jersey. My address is c/o Mr. J. Alfred Harris, RD 1, Grover's Corner, Princeton, N.J. 08540. If I should lose this journal, and anyone finds it, please mail it back to me. I will pay you back for the postage.

The reason I am spending the summer with my aunt and uncle is that my father is in the diplomatic service and we have lived abroad most of my life. Two years ago my dad and mom decided it would be a good idea if I spent my summers in the United States.

"You are being culturally deprived," my father said.

"I'm not a bit worried that you are missing all those silly so-called comedies on TV, or the cartoons, or the advertising. But a normal American boy ought to see a few big-league baseball games and occasionally eat a real American hamburger and drink a genuine milk shake. And I've noticed that quite a few foreign words have crept into your speech. That's okay, but you are probably way out of touch with current American slang. You won't be able to understand what the average American kid is saying unless we do something."

I think Dad was wrong about the slang because American slang gets all over the world pretty fast. But he was certainly right about the hamburgers and milk shakes. We were living in Italy when I came over to New Jersey the first time. You can't get a really good hamburger with relish and ketchup and onions and everything in Italy or anyplace else in Europe. As for a good thick milk shake—forget it! For that matter you can't get a pizza in Rome that is nearly as good as the pizzas you can get almost anywhere in the United States. For a full-course dinner, Italy is great, but when it comes to pizzas, the Italians have a lot to learn. I said to Dad that I thought the reason was that all the good pizza makers in Italy had moved to the United States to open pizza parlors. I suggested our State Department could build some international goodwill by sending a mission back to Italy to teach them to make good pizzas. He didn't seem to think much of that idea and I doubt if he even took it up with the State Department in Washington.

I began spending my summers in Grover's Corner when

we were living in Italy. My father is now at the embassy in Manila. This is my third summer here. Spending the summer out in the country is fun even if there aren't many kids to play with. There is really only one person anywhere near my age in Grover's Corner and that is a girl named Margaret Glass. Her nickname is Midge. Midge acts crazy at times but she is smart and you can depend on her. She is not the giggly sort that some girls are or else she's past that stage. She and I have been partners in several things and have become good friends. We had a research business, we ran a baby-sitting service, and we just put on a big rodeo. Midge isn't here now because she is visiting an aunt in Washington, D.C., for a few days.

I also have a dog named Agony. Agony is a beagle who sort of adopted me the first summer I came here. I don't really know if he's my dog now or Uncle Al and Aunt Mabel's, since they have become very fond of him. He spends a lot more of the year with them than he does with me. However, he always knows me and carries on like crazy when I come back for the summer.

It has been raining all day and everybody has been cooped up in the house. Aunt Mabel wanted to go outside and work in her flower garden, Uncle Al wanted to do something with his tomatoes, and I guess Agony wanted to go chase a rabbit. Instead Aunt Mabel puttered around in the kitchen, Uncle Al did something in his workshop, and Agony slept. I found a good book.

About seven in the evening the telephone rang. It was my mother calling from Manila. Of course it was seven in the morning out there. It was great to hear her voice. I told her all about what I had been doing and she told me what had been happening there. The most important news was about school. It is going to start late, maybe not until the first of October. We don't have a very big American school in Manila and a missing teacher is really missed. One of our teachers broke his leg while he was back in the United States for the summer. Now it seems another one has a very sick mother and doesn't know when she will be able to go back. They have to find one temporary replacement and one permanent one, so school will start late.

"What would you like to do?" Mom asked. "Come back September 3 as you planned, or stay two or three weeks longer?"

I didn't want to hurt her feelings, but I like Grover's Corner better than I like Manila. "Well, I'd like to see you and Dad but there won't be much happening out there," I said. I looked outside and there wasn't much happening in Grover's Corner either, except a steady drizzle. But things change fast around here. "I'd just as soon stay here a while."

Her feelings weren't hurt a bit. "Well, if that is what you prefer we'll see if your Aunt Mabel is willing to put up with you for a bit longer. I will probably go to India with your father. They have a special project there and they would like his help for a few weeks. Let me speak to Mabel for a few minutes, Henry."

She talked to Aunt Mabel, who said she would be delighted to have me stay several weeks longer. Then Mom talked to Uncle Al, who is her older brother.

"Well, he seems to find things to do," Uncle Al said in answer to some question. "And Grover's Corner isn't such a quiet place these days. It's more like it used to be when you were a kid—stirring everything to a boil." There was a pause while he listened to something Mom said. "Yes, I suppose school will start here at the usual time and his partner Midge will be gone during the day. But don't worry about it. The schoolhouse will blow up or there will be a flood or something to liven things a bit."

Uncle Al talks in riddles a lot of the time, but Mom seems to understand him. Anyhow, it was settled that I would stay on several weeks longer than originally planned.

"Well, you've got a whole month left," Uncle Al said as we were having dinner a few minutes later. "What are you going to do with all that time? Got any new projects in mind?"

"Not really," I said. I thought about it for a minute. School would be starting fairly early in September for all the kids who lived in the Princeton area, and I wouldn't have anyone my age around during the day.

"I might start up my research business again," I said. "But the research Midge and I were doing two years ago was sort of kids' stuff, and I'm way past that now. I wouldn't mind doing some atomic research but the equipment I'd need might be pretty expensive."

"So I understand," Uncle Al said. Uncle Al likes to emphasize an important point by waving his fork if he's at the table. The trouble is that there is often something on the fork. This time it was a piece of steak. "You might be able to get a secondhand atom smasher from Princeton

7

University for $25 or $30 million. But the cost isn't the problem. You could probably get a government grant. The big hitch is that people who live in Grover's Corner might object to your making the area an atomic research center."

"Cost is a big problem with me," I said. "Suppose I wanted to do something simple like research about dog foods—what food is best and liked best by beagles. I would need test tubes, chemicals, and a can of every kind of dog food in the supermarket. I went shopping with Aunt Mabel the other day and she told me to get Agony some canned dog food. Why, there are dozens and dozens. Even if I could afford one can of every kind it would take forever with only one beagle. I'd have to have another dog."

"Let's cross that one off," Aunt Mabel said. "One dog is enough."

Uncle Al looked at the piece of steak on the end of his fork as though he had just discovered it.

"I've got it!" he said. "Just turn your research organization into a think tank. There would be no expense and you and Midge are eminently qualified to be think-tank experts."

"What is a think tank?" I asked.

"A think tank is a group of supposedly very wise individuals who sit around and think and solve problems. I don't know how wise they really are, but they are smart enough to get some very fancy fees for their thinking."

"That sounds interesting," I said. Uncle Al has some great ideas. "We wouldn't need any laboratory equipment at all."

Uncle Al shook his head. "None. Nothing except a good brain, a quiet spot where you can think, a chair to sit on while you are thinking and maybe a scratch pad and pencil. You've got everything except the scratch pad and I will be glad to donate that. Your barn would be a perfect spot for a think tank."

Uncle Al always calls it "my barn," but it is really my mother's. There is a three-acre lot a short distance up the road from Uncle Al's house. There was once a house there, and Uncle Al and my mother grew up in it. The house burned down years ago and my mother now owns the land. She says that someday, when my dad retires, they will build a house there. The only building there now is a small barn near the road. Last summer Midge Glass and I used it for our baby-sitting service, and the year before that for our research center. Midge lives right across the road from it. We have an old desk and three chairs in the barn. I don't know where the desk came from but the chairs are from Midge's attic.

"Where could I find out more about think tanks?"

"I read an article about think tanks earlier this week," he said. "I've forgotten where. But in the morning when I go to the office you can go with me and we'll stop at the library. They will have it. It was in one of the weekly news magazines."

Monday, August 19

*I went to Princeton this morning with Uncle Al. Princeton
has a very nice library and the librarians are helpful. We
found the article Uncle Al mentioned. I stayed in the
library to read it while Uncle Al went on to his office.
One of the librarians found a second article in a magazine
and a chapter in a book called "Consulting—A Growth
Industry."*

It seems there are hundreds and hundreds of consulting
firms in the United States. Most of them are consultants
for business, although the government in Washington uses
lots of consultants too. Consulting firms specialize in all
sorts of fields like energy, mining, or banking. When they
solve general problems they seem to be called think tanks.
They think about such things as what policy we should

follow in Central America or how to get people back to using trains again to commute. Think tanks solve all sorts of problems, and since our government in Washington has all sorts of problems, most think tanks work for the government.

I spent several hours in the library and then walked over to Uncle Al's office and rode back with him to Grover's Corner for lunch.

"Well, did you learn all about think tanks?" Uncle Al asked as we were riding along.

"I learned quite a bit," I said. "But I've got two questions."

"I don't claim to be a think tank myself, but I'll answer them if I can. Shoot."

"Why is the government or a business willing to spend a lot of money for advice when there is so much free advice around?"

"A good question," Uncle Al said. "Especially good, as I think I can answer it. Most people think that anything that is free isn't worth much. Often that is wrong but when it comes to advice it is usually right. Let me ask you a question. What adults always seem to know the most and are the quickest to offer advice on how to bring up children?"

I didn't have to think long. "People like the Apples down the road from us. They don't have any children."

"Exactly right," Uncle Al said. "What's the other question?"

"Well, that article listed lots of outfits that were think tanks according to the author. But none of them called themselves "think tanks." They all have names like the Hudson Institute, the Johns Hopkins International Institute, or the Kennan Center for Advanced Study—big fancy names. Why is that?"

"Just putting on the dog," Uncle Al said. "Dressing themselves up. Why do garbage men call themselves sanitation workers when everyone up and down the street calls them garbage men? Adults like titles, Henry. Did you ever look at the list of titles at a good-sized bank? Almost everyone except the janitor is at least a vice president. Well, what have you decided after your studies in the library? Are you going to start your own think tank?"

"I might," I said. "But if I do I am going to call it a plain old think tank."

"Good for you," Uncle Al said. "I predict being direct and honest will bring you business."

Tuesday, August 20

Being honest and direct may bring me lots of business, as Uncle Al says, but being efficient and planning ahead hasn't done much for me except to cause trouble and bring complaints.

I woke up early this morning. It was a beautiful sunny day, so I got dressed very quietly and went down to let Agony out for a run. There's not much traffic in Grover's Corner, especially very early in the morning, so you don't have to keep a dog on a leash. Besides, beagles are smart, and Agony is smart even for a beagle. He knows enough to keep out of the way of cars. He went sniffing around in the garden and then took off down the side of the road toward the barn. I wasn't worried, but I decided to follow him.

He disappeared into the underbrush just as I reached the barn. I stood there for a minute looking up at the sign on the end of the barn facing the road. It reads:

REED AND GLASS
ENTERPRISES INC.

The letters are almost a foot high and are white, while the barn is a faded red. That sign took a lot of work to paint and it is still in pretty good shape. If Midge wanted to be a partner in the think tank all I needed to do was to repaint the second line and touch up the top line a bit. If she didn't stay a partner, I'd have to repaint the first line also. The sensible thing to do was to repaint the second line and wait and see before I did anything more.

Agony showed up and so we went back to the house. I went down in the basement and hunted through Uncle Al's supply of half-used paint. I found a can of white and some red that would do. Then I smelled bacon so I hurried upstairs for breakfast.

Uncle Al said it was all right to use the paint so after breakfast I carried a ladder down to the barn and painted out the second line of the sign. I let it dry until after lunch and then roughed in my new words, THINK TANK. I painted them carefully in white and touched up a couple of letters in the top line. I'm pretty good at lettering and the sign looked fine when I had finished. I took the ladder down and was about to carry it back when Midge appeared. I hadn't known she was back. She was eating an apple, just as she had been when I first met her a couple of years ago.

"Hi," she said. She looked up at the sign. "What's this think-tank stuff?"

"Well, I've been doing some serious thinking about our research business," I said. "We never got much business and to get any now we'd need to specialize. And we'd need a lot of expensive equipment. But a think tank just needs brains and we have two of those. So I decided to convert our organization into a think tank."

"*You* decided!" Midge said. She took a vicious bite of her apple. "There are two brains involved in this business and this brain isn't certain it wants to be part of a think tank, whatever that is. I thought I was a partner! Whatever happened to women's rights in this firm? You are a male chauvinist, Henry Reed."

I wasn't sure what a male chauvinist was but I didn't think I would like it when I found out. I got annoyed too.

"And you are a women's-lib lunatic," I said in a very dignified voice. "You didn't let me finish what I was saying."

"Finish," she said coldly.

"You don't have to be part of any think tank," I said. "But I am starting one. I was being thoughtful and considerate. I was waiting to find out if you wanted to join me before I painted out the top line and changed it to HENRY REED."

I put the ladder back against the barn, picked up the red paint, and began climbing.

She waited until I got all the way to the top. "I'll give it some thought," she said. "Right now I've got to go home. My aunt will be leaving in a minute and I want to say goodbye. I had a good time in Washington. I met a senator. If I do decide to join your think tank, I might be able to get us a government contract."

I took down the ladder again and carried it and the paint back to the house. You can never be certain about Midge, but I figured she would probably stay in the partnership. I went back to the barn and began cleaning things up a bit. The old desk and the chairs had a thick layer of dust on them. I had swept out and was rearranging things to make the place look more like an office when Midge came back.

"We've got problems if we want people to think we have an honest-to-goodness think tank," she announced.

"What kind of problems?"

"I asked my Dad about them," she said. "He knows quite a bit about them because there are two or three in Princeton. He says people in think tanks either have a fancy college degree, a big bushy beard, or a huge stomach. A lot of them have all three. We haven't got any of those things, so we wouldn't impress anyone very much if he was looking around for a think tank."

I thought about that for a minute. "We'll go after younger clients. They aren't so impressed by big stomachs or beards or college degrees."

"That's true," Midge admitted. "They don't know what a Ph.D. is. But there's another problem I didn't mention. Dad said a good think tank usually has a whole board or panel of experts. There's just two of us. Two can't be called a panel or group. They're just a pair."

Just then Agony came around the corner of the barn.

He looked up at the sign, cocked his head to one side, and then scratched his right ear with his right hind leg.

"We'll add Agony to our firm. He can be a limited partner."

"What's a limited partner?" she asked. "If that means someone with limited intelligence, maybe we all of us ought to be limited partners." She seemed to think that was very funny but I didn't. I could see that there would be a few problems with Midge on the staff. From what I had read, people in think tanks are very serious people who always act as though they know the answer to everything. They don't make silly jokes.

"Well, are you joining me or not?" I asked. "And if you do, what do you want to be? Vice president?"

"I suppose you will be president?" she asked, looking up at the tree tops and putting on an innocent act.

I figured she was about to pull something. After all it was my barn and my idea in the first place so I figured I ought to be president. However, since she had brought up all that stuff about women's rights, I decided it would be best to be diplomatic. And I did want her to be part of my think tank. Midge is a year younger than I am and she acts a little juvenile at times but she is smart and we get along well most of the time.

"Would you like to be president?" I asked.

"No, I think you'd make a great president," she said, smiling very sweetly. "I vote for you for president. I guess I can have any of the titles left over. Okay?"

"Sure," I said. "Anything you want."

"Then I'll be treasurer," she said. "Maybe I'll be secretary and treasurer. I'll use an English accent. I read someplace that all high-powered business executives have an English secretary to answer the telephone."

"The person with the title of secretary in a company is an officer of the firm. A plain secretary is someone who answers the phone and types and things like that," I said. "They are different."

"I'll be both," Midge said. "When I answer the phone as an ordinary secretary, I'll have a refined English accent, don't you know, old chap. When I answer the phone as an officer, I'll have a real bossy accent."

"Be serious. We don't have a phone, and until we make some money we can't afford one."

"But if I join the firm, and I haven't absolutely decided yet, we will have a telephone," she said. "We have one of those cordless phones at our house. My Dad got it last spring. The idea was that he would take it outside when he was working in the garden. But he never uses it, especially during the week when he's at work. It will work fine from here. I figure that is just about as important a contribution as your barn."

Her telephone idea was a good one, I had to admit. Whether it was as important as the barn or not was another matter. We began to talk about stationery and decided we could rake up enough money between us to get some printed. Midge said she knew a printer who was cheap. Soon she was more enthusiastic about the think tank than I was. I think she wanted the stationery to write to a couple of friends who had moved to Kansas. She wanted to impress them, I guess, but I didn't say anything. We were deciding how our stationery should look when I saw some-one padding down the road toward us. He was lumbering along, and even from a distance you could tell he wasn't enjoying himself.

"Here comes a jogger with purple pants," I said.

Midge looked up. "Wow!" she said. "Be right back."

She dashed across the street and disappeared in her house. A minute later she came running back again with a camera in her hand.

The jogger was quite close by this time. It was a boy, probably about my age and height, but he was fat! He had legs that would have looked better on a grand piano, a real fat behind, fat arms, and a fat face. His face was wet with perspiration and he had that look of agony that most joggers have. They all seem to be in pain and they act like their next step will be their last.

In addition to his purple shorts, this jogger was wearing a bright green T-shirt with a big pink star on the chest, and a yellow band or ribbon around his forehead.

"Glad I had color film in the camera," Midge said.

She stepped out to the side of the road as the jogger got close and snapped a picture. "Hi, Rodney," she said.

He came to a stop. "Why'd you take my picture?" he asked, puffing between each word.

"I'm making a collection of pictures of joggers' cos-tumes. I started in Washington, D.C. Boy, did I get some great ones there!"

Rodney looked down at his chest. "What do you think of mine?" he asked proudly.

"Very striking," Midge said. "And colorful. Maybe when

I get a big collection I'll have a one-woman show. I'll bet the Squibb Gallery over on Route 206 would be happy to display them. When it happens I'll let you know, Rodney. You'll be in it in full color."

"Thanks," Rodney said. He sounded as though he meant it. The only thing I can say about his costume is that someone in a car couldn't help seeing him. He wasn't puffing so hard by this time but he didn't seem too anxious to get back to his jogging. Midge noticed the same thing.

"Don't let us interrupt your jogging," she said, closing her camera.

"You're not really interrupting. Maybe I've jogged far enough for today anyhow. Jogging is hard work."

"How long you been doing it?" I asked.

"This is my second day."

"What are you trying to do? Take off some of that flab?" Midge asked. It's easy sometimes to tell Midge's parents aren't in the diplomatic service.

Rodney looked pained. "I was just getting in shape."

"For what?" Midge insisted.

"Just for anything that came along," he said. He looked up at our sign. "What does a think tank do?"

"Solve problems," I said. "We get the facts, think about the problem, do whatever research we need to do, and come up with the best solution."

"For a fee," Midge added.

He seemed quite impressed. "Do you really? What kind of problems?"

"Well, we don't do much in the engineering, chemical, or scientific fields," I said. "We leave that sort of problems

20

to Ph.D.s with big stomachs. We stick to problems involving people."

"Gee," he said, very impressed now. "Can you solve difficult ones?"

I didn't know how to answer that question but Midge did. She stuck her chin in the air and said, "We haven't failed yet."

"Well I've got a problem," Rodney said. He sounded miserable. "Do you suppose you could solve it?"

"Why don't you tell us about it?" I said. We didn't have even a pencil in the office, much less a pad of paper. However, my Uncle Al says that when you have a live client, hold on to him. I figured we had better hold on to Rodney.

"Come on into the office and we'll make a few notes." I looked at Midge. "I guess you took your note pad home with you at lunch."

"Righto," Midge said in her terrible British accent. "I'll run over and get it."

A couple of minutes later we were all in the office. Midge had a pencil in her hand and a notebook on her knee. All I saw her do was wet the end of the pencil now and then and doodle on her pad. But it looked good, and Rodney was so full of his problem that he didn't notice whether she really took notes or not.

"My dad is a great athlete," Rodney said sadly. "He always has been. When he went to high school out in Ohio he was on the basketball team, he was the captain of his football team, and he was a track star. When he went to Lehigh he was on the football team there and the track team too. He won all sorts of varsity letters. He's good at tennis now and beats most of the people he plays. He's a fine skier, he can really swim, and is great at diving."

"You must be proud of him," I said.

"Well, I am," Rodney said. "But he's not very proud of me. I'm not good at any sport. Dad is always trying to coach me so I'll be good in something or other." Rodney sighed. "I guess I'm just a big disappointment."

"Couldn't you pick just one sport and do it well?" Midge asked.

"There are sports where a little extra weight doesn't bother you too much," I suggested. "How are you at swimming?"

"Well, I float pretty good," Rodney said. "But who ever heard of a floating contest?"

"Do you want to be in a contest?" I asked.

"Yes, I'd like to win some medal or prize or something," he said sadly. "I heard my dad talking to my mother one day and he said he wished I would get interested in something and learn to do it well—just anything."

"You must be interested in something," I said. "No hobbies?"

"I'm not interested in any sports," he said. "I don't even watch football or baseball on TV. I do have some hobbies, though."

"Such as?"

"Well, I like to read. I like to watch birds and I know a lot about them. I'm a pretty good photographer. And I am a real expert at grilling hamburgers and steaks." He paused and thought a minute. "I'm pretty good at jigsaw puzzles."

"Very useful accomplishments," Midge said, sympathetically. "But almost all of them are fattening."

Rodney nodded miserably.

"Let's see if we've got your problem straight," I said. "You'd like to be really good at something and win a contest with lots of publicity so that your dad would be proud of you."

"Yeah, I guess that's about it," Rodney said. "I've thought and thought and thought and it's no use. So I figured that while I was trying to think of something I would jog and get in shape for anything that might come up." He got to his feet, looking miserable. "But I hate jogging!"

"We'll think about your problem," I said. "We'll get our whole staff working on it and try to come up with an answer."

"I hope you can," Rodney said hopefully. "I'd appreciate it."

"That brings up one final point," Midge said, looking up from her doodling. "There's a fee for our services if we come up with an answer."

"Well, I have a pretty good allowance," Rodney said. "I don't have any money right now, but I could pay you gradually—you know, installments."

"How much a week?" Midge asked.

"I guess I could give you a dollar a week," Rodney said, looking as though he had a bad stomachache. "I'd have to do without ice-cream cones and candy, I guess."

"That would be satisfactory," Midge announced. "Do you good to cut out ice cream and candy, anyhow. How many weeks you will have to pay depends on how much work we have to do and how successful we are."

She made some notes on her pad and I could see that she wasn't doodling this time.

"Well, I'd better be going," Rodney said. He started toward the road and then turned. "I forgot one thing. I make good kites and they can really fly."

He went padding down the road the way he had come. He didn't look as though he was enjoying it.

"Rodney must have a nice allowance if he can afford to pay us a dollar a week out of it," Midge said thoughtfully. "That would mean our firm could pay both the president and the treasurer fifty cents in expense money each week."

"If we can come up with some sort of answer to his problem," I said. "And that's a big if. We better think about it for a while and then have a conference."

"I've thought about it," Midge said. "It's hopeless."

"Why?"

"I've known Rodney for years. He's always eating, and he's always been fat. And he is always going to do something about it, like going on a diet or jogging, but he gives up after a few days. You know he's never going to do anything athletic with all that flab."

"Maybe he could do something that isn't athletic," I suggested. "What's his father like? Would he be pleased if Rodney won some sort of mental competition? Say a chess championship?"

"His father's nice enough, and I think he'd be tickled pink if Rodney was a chess champion. But Rodney doesn't play chess. I happen to know, because he's in several classes of mine at school and for some reason one of our teachers asked one day if any of us played chess. Only one student did and he wasn't Rodney. We don't have anything to work with, Henry. He reads and he watches birds. It would be pretty hard to have an exciting contest doing either one of those. As for photography, forget it! With the cameras you can get today anyone who doesn't stick his finger in front of the lens can take great pictures. Besides, there are photographic contests all over the place. People are fed up with them. What else did he say he did?"

"Grill hamburgers and do jigsaw puzzles."

"Rodney thinks all food is delicious because he is always hungry," Midge said. "I wouldn't bet on his being able to grill any better hamburgers than my dad, and he burns ours half the time. And can you imagine a jigsaw-puzzle contest?" She shook her head. "Much as I'd like that fifty cents a week, I think we better forget him. If we have a big fat failure on our first job, think what it will do to our reputation. I vote we tell him to go fly his kites and we spend our time looking for better clients."

I thought about that for a minute. I hated to lose our very first client or give up on our first job.

"Maybe that is it," I said. "We could have a big kite-flying contest. Advertise it and make a big thing of it."

Midge was quiet for several minutes. Then a big smile lighted up her face. "That's a brilliant idea! Rodney does make great kites and he knows how to fly them. I can see it all now—a huge crowd out in Mr. Baines's pasture, the sky all filled with brightly colored kites, people cheering, newspaper people snapping pictures, the band playing, and Rodney being awarded the prize. You and I can both make speeches. It'll be terrific."

One nice thing about Midge is that she recognizes a brilliant idea when she hears one. And it wasn't a bad idea the way she described it. Of course, she gets too enthusiastic and goes overboard now and then. We didn't have a chance of getting a band to come play at something like a kite-flying contest, but I didn't say anything.

"All right, I've decided," Midge said. "I will be a member of the think tank. I predict a great future for it."

Wednesday, August 21

Business is picking up. We got a second client today. Our think tank is already becoming well known in this part of New Jersey.

Midge and I went to Princeton this morning. Mrs. Glass wanted to do some shopping, so Midge and I went along. Midge went to see the printer about our stationery and I went to the library to read about kites. If we are going to have a great kite-flying contest, we need to know something about kites. I found a lot about how to make kites and about different kinds of kites, more than I needed to know, but nothing about the rules and regulations for kite-flying contests. Maybe no one ever had one. I'll do some more research, but it looks as though we can make any rules we want.

We got back to Grover's Corner about eleven o'clock to find a girl sitting on her bicycle in front of the barn. She looked as though she was about to leave, so we hurried over to talk to her.

"Know her?" I asked Midge as we crossed the road.

"I've seen her around but I don't know her," Midge said. "I think she lives over toward Lawrenceville."

"You waiting to see us?" I asked as we got near.

She nodded. "I guess so, if you are the think-tank people," the girl said. Or at least I guess that is what she said. She mumbled so that I wasn't certain.

She was a small, skinny girl with dark brown, almost black eyes that stared at us without blinking through big, black-rimmed spectacles. She had a big nose and ears that stuck out. Her hair was long and done up in a bun right on the top of her head. She sounds awful-looking, but after you have talked to her for a few minutes you forget all about her looks. She is smart. I guess she is about twelve.

"You are in luck," Midge said. "We are the think-tank people and we have just returned from doing some research. Come on in."

The girl got off her bicycle, leaned it against the barn, and followed us inside.

"What's your name?" Midge asked, pushing a chair toward her.

The girl mumbled something that sounded like "Dee-dee" or "Dreamy."

"I'm sorry, but I didn't catch the name," I said politely.

"Dreedree," she mumbled. I decided she must be tongue-tied, or have some sort of a speech defect. I still didn't know what her name was.

Midge leaned forward and looked at the girl closely. "If we are going to get anywhere, you'd better take that wad of gum out of your mouth," she said. "We can't understand a word you say."

The girl took the biggest wad of gum I have ever seen from her mouth, and calmly stuck it behind her right ear. It stuck out even further than the ear.

"Does it ever get in your hair?" Midge asked.

"Not when I have my hair up this way." Without the gum the girl spoke quite clearly.

"What is your name again?" I asked.

"Deirdre."

"Deirdre what?" Midge asked.

"Deirdre Mullins."

Midge wrote down the girl's name, address, and telephone number, and then said, "Now what is the problem?"

"My allowance," Deirdre said promptly. "It isn't nearly enough."

"Allowances never are," I said. "How much is yours?"

"A mere thirty-five cents a week," Deirdre said scornfully. "I've asked my father for more and he refuses."

"It isn't much," I agreed. "But maybe it's all he can afford."

"Isn't much!" Midge said indignantly. "Why she'd have to save almost three months to go to a movie! She's poverty stricken!"

"He can afford more," Deirdre said flatly. "I guess

29

we're not what you'd call rich but we aren't poor either. Dad admits he could pay me more than thirty-five cents."

"What is he, just plain stingy?" Midge asked. Midge has a knack of coming right to the point.

"No, he's a great father," Deirdre said. "And he's generous about most things. But he says he is a businessman, and I haven't shown him any economic justification for a raise. He says I am well fed, have all my clothes bought for me, don't have to buy gasoline or pay income taxes, and even have my bicycle repairs paid for. He says if I can give him any sort of proof that I should be paid more, then he'll give it to me."

"What about your mother?" Midge asked. "Is she on your side?"

"She says it is my problem," Deirdre replied. "She's in business too. She has an antique shop. Both of them say it is a straight business proposition. I have to come up with facts."

"That's a bit hard to do if they buy everything for you," I pointed out.

"But they don't buy everything," Deirdre said indignantly. "There are lots of little things. Gum, for instance. My allowance barely covers my gum."

"I can believe that," Midge said, looking at the huge wad of gum that was still stuck behind Deirdre's ear. It looked as though it might become unstuck at any minute.

"Have you tried anything except just asking for more money?" I asked.

"Several things," Deirdre said. "I tried wearing the oldest and raggedest clothes I could find. Blue jeans with big holes in them, T-shirts messed up with paint, clothes that showed how poor I was. Dad and Mom both offered to take me shopping. Then I opened a lemonade stand in front of our house. Dad offered to lend me money to buy more lemons. But I didn't do much business at the stand. Traffic moves too fast past our house. No one walks along the road and most cars are afraid of stopping. Then I tried to get jobs baby-sitting, but most folks think I'm younger than I really am. Besides, we haven't many close neighbors and I don't know many people who need baby-sitters."

"I'd say you've tried," Midge said sympathetically.

"I've tried everything I know. So when my friend Rodney said you two had a think tank, I decided to come see you. He says you two are very smart."

"We have solved some very difficult problems," Midge said with a wave of her hand. I guess she was referring to some of the problems we had had in our other businesses. "By the way, how would you be able to pay us if we solved your problem? Out of your bigger allowance?"

"Oh, no. In cash," Deirdre said. "I have some money. I have a bank account with quite a bit in it that my grandmother has given me. I'm saving that until I go to college. I don't want to spend it on things like bubble gum, ice-cream cones, and the movies."

"Would you spend some of it to pay us?" Midge asked.

"Oh, sure," Deirdre said. "If I pay you for getting me a bigger allowance that is sort of an investment, you see."

"Exactly," I agreed.

"Well, what do you think, Henry?" Midge asked. "Can we fit Deirdre's problem into our schedule?"

I had been thinking about her problem, and I had a couple of ideas. "We might," I said, trying to look very serious and wise. It wasn't easy because by this time the wad of gum was almost ready to drop and I couldn't keep my eyes off it. I understand now why Mr. Glass had said it helped in the think-tank business to have a big bushy beard. People can't tell then if you keep your face straight or not.

"You are about to lose your gum," Midge said, ruining everything.

"Thanks," Deirdre said, resetting the gum behind her ear. "I'd hate to lose that, it's almost fresh. At least some of it is. What do you think we might try?"

"My first idea would be the quickest and easiest, if it works. Does your father work around here?" I asked.

"He has a plastics plant over on Route 1," Deirdre said. "He's the president."

"Good," I said. "We could picket the place. All three of us with signs saying he was unfair to you."

"Not bad at all," Midge said. "I can think of some lulus of signs. Mullins unfair to children—discrimination against women—unfair to minors—down with starvation allowances. All sorts of important businessmen probably come to see your father and there we'd be, marching in front of the office with our signs."

Deirdre shook her head. "Don't like it."

"Would you feel silly carrying a big placard?" Midge asked.

"Oh, no. That would be fun. But I don't think it would work. My dad is stubborn, and besides he might put someone out to picket *us*. Picketing is sort of like blackmail anyhow."

"That's true," I admitted. "Maybe you will like my second idea. We will do a study or poll of people with children in this area. We'll find out how much most kids get for an allowance. If we find out that you are way below average, we will write up a report showing that to your father."

"I like that," Deirdre said. "That might work. I'm sure I'm way below average."

Agony got up from where he had been sleeping in the corner and went outside. Midge looked at him and said, "We'll take it up with the entire staff, and if everyone agrees, we'll go ahead with the survey."

Deirdre popped her gum back in her mouth, mumbled something that I couldn't understand, and left.

"Two customers already," I said. "I think we should start on her case first. Organizing a kite-flying contest is going to take time, but we can start on this as soon as we draw up a list of questions."

"That's not so easy," Midge warned. "It happens that I am sort of an expert on opinion polls. At least compared to the other members of our think tank."

"Why?" I asked doubtfully.

"Princeton is crawling with pollsters," Midge said. "And the vice president of one of the big polling firms happens to be a friend of my dad's. He and his wife come over for dinner now and then and I hear a lot of talk about how to take polls. To get the answers you want you have to slant the questions just right."

"What do you mean?"

"Suppose you ask the question: Should teachers enforce order and attention in the classroom? What answer would you get?"

"Yes," I said.

"All right. Suppose you asked: Should teachers wallop an unruly pupil over the head with a textbook if he won't pay attention? What answer would you get?"

"Yes, if it was my mother they asked and the teacher was talking about me," I said. "But I get the idea."

We sat down with a pad of yellow paper and in about fifteen minutes we had a list of questions. Midge is a smart girl and she thought of most of the questions. What we needed to know in the very beginning was if the person being interviewed had any children near our age. If they didn't, they probably had no idea of the problems our generation faces. This was our final list:

1. Do you have children?
2. What are the ages of these children?
3. Do you give them an allowance?
4. How much is this allowance per week?
5. Do you think spending his own money helps a child learn how to handle money properly?
6. Do you think allowing a child to buy some of his or her own clothes or school supplies will teach the child how to shop and know values?
7. Do you think if a child has an allowance much smaller than that of his or her friends it will cause problems of adjustment?

8. Do you think a child's allowance should be adjusted now and then to keep up with inflation?
9. Do you think if a child is allowed to buy and pay for an item such as a sweater it will cost more or less than if he or she picks it out and you pay for it?

"Number seven is a dilly," Midge said. "Of course having too small an allowance causes problems of adjustment. The way the average kid adjusts is to mow lawns or baby-sit to earn more money. But we won't mention that."

It clouded up while we were working on our questions, so we put off starting the actual work until the next day.

Thursday, August 22

We began taking our poll today, and I guess we finished too. Asking people the same questions over and over gets sort of tiresome. But when it was all over we had learned quite a bit about allowances and a lot about people. One thing we know: we don't want to be poll takers as a permanent job. It was a long, hot, dull day. There was some excitement toward the end, which helped a bit, though. Midge and I happened to see it all from start to finish so I'm writing down what happened while I remember it all clearly. After all, if anyone sues anyone else Midge or I might be called as a witness.

Mrs. Glass dropped us in Princeton a few blocks from the shopping center. We picked a street and started down it, ringing every doorbell. It was only a few minutes after nine o'clock, but it was already hot and sticky. We didn't get much done at first. Some people weren't home, a lot who were home were very slow in answering their doorbells and of course at least half of those we talked to had no children anywhere near our age. A few people slammed the door in our faces, but most people were polite and helpful.

The poll would have gone much faster if we could have worked separately, but we had promised Mrs. Glass that we would stay together. "There are weird people in this world, and I don't think it is wise for children your age to be ringing doorbells of strangers alone. Stay together."

Toward the end of the second block we found out what she meant. We were taking turns—one of us asking the questions and the other one writing down the answers. It was Midge's turn to ask questions. A big hulking man, maybe fifty or sixty, answered the doorbell. He had a big bushy beard, bushy hair, and fierce eyes.

"Good morning," Midge said politely. "We are taking a poll about children's allowances. Do you have any children?"

"I do," he growled in a deep voice. "And I don't believe in making any allowances for children, regardless of age." He glared first at Midge and then at me.

"Oh," Midge said weakly. "How old is your child or children?"

"Immaterial!" he bellowed. "I am a poet and my opinion of children can best be expressed in the words of a great poet:

Speak roughly to your little boy
And beat him when he sneezes
He only does it to annoy
Because he knows it teases.

"Do you know who wrote those beautiful words?" he asked Midge, glaring at her.

My father thought *Alice in Wonderland* was the greatest book ever written and he read it to me at least six times, so I knew the answer.

"It's from *Alice in Wonderland*," I said.

"And Lewis Carroll wrote it," Midge added immediately.

"Right!" he roared. "You two restore my faith in the younger generation. Sit down." He waved his hand at some chairs on the big front porch. "You both look hot. I will get us all a cold Coke."

He disappeared and returned a minute later with three bottles of Coca-Cola. They were cold and tasted good.

"I don't have any children except a grown daughter," he said. "But I'd like to hear about this poll of yours."

We explained a bit about why we were taking the poll and the questions that we were asking.

"Good creative thinking," he said. "How's it going?"

"Very slow," Midge said. "Too many people aren't home or they don't have children our age."

"I have a suggestion," he said. "Go over to the shopping center. You know where it is?"

"Yes," Midge said.

"Good. Wait outside the supermarket. When the women

come out with their carts of groceries you can get a good idea if they have children about your age. All that junk food in the carts will tell you. And the number of bags is a good indication. If the cart is bulging there are probably three or four hungry youngsters at home. And of course you can ask. That way you won't have to ring any doorbells."

"That sounds like a great idea," I said.

We thanked him for the Coca-Cola and walked over to the shopping center. His suggestion was perfect. In the next half hour we polled more people than we had all morning ringing doorbells. And he was right about the groceries. You could tell almost every time by what was in the cart whether there were children in the family. We figured out a system that worked like a charm. I would offer to wheel the cart to the car and load the groceries into the trunk or back seat if the woman would answer Midge's questions. We polled more than twenty people and then there was a short lull. Midge called her mother from a pay phone. Mrs. Glass said she would pick us up in about half an hour.

We went to the delicatessen and bought sandwiches and cold drinks. Then we went outside and sat on the grass at the edge of the parking lot.

There are several tennis courts not too far from the shopping center. I think they belong to the school. Two girls in white tennis outfits were playing while a third one watched. We were half watching them when a big golden retriever came trotting up to us. He was carrying a tattered old tennis ball in his mouth which he put down at my feet.

"That's Herbert," Midge said. "Herbert likes you to throw his tennis ball. He chases it and brings it back. He never gets tired of the game. But you have to watch because once he starts to chase the ball he never sees anything else. He will run right in front of a car."

"Whose dog is he?" I asked. He seemed very friendly.

"I don't know," Midge said. "But I know the house where he belongs. He's well known around this neighborhood but this is the first time I have seen him here at the shopping center. I have a girlfriend who lives over on the opposite side of the center. Two or three times when I've been at Lily's house Herbert has shown up with his tennis ball." Midge looked over at the three girls playing tennis. "I think that is Lily's older sister—the tall one with a ponytail."

Herbert nudged me and rolled the ball a little closer. I picked it up and threw it out on the grass, away from the cars. He was after it like a flash and in a minute had brought it back and put it down again. I threw it five or six times more, eating my sandwich between throws. We finished our drinks and took our empty cans and papers over to a trash bin. Herbert trotted along, carrying his ball. He kept nudging me to get me to throw it again. I pretended not to see him because I didn't want to throw the ball across the asphalt parking lot. Some car might run over him.

The three girls finished their tennis match and started across the shopping-center parking lot.

"That *is* Lily's sister," Midge said. "Hi, Gussie!" she called.

Gussie pretended she didn't hear her.

"Hi, Gussie," Midge called again. "It's me, Midge."

A car drove up and parked very near the three girls. Whoever was driving was a friend of the other two tennis players and they went over to say hello. Gussie didn't go with them but came over toward us.

"My name is not Gussie!" she said in a furious voice. "And I will thank you not to yell at me, you brat!"

She turned and went on toward the supermarket. The other two girls finished talking and caught up with her. Just outside the supermarket exit they met a tall young man coming out with a bag in his arms. They must have thought he was wonderful because they clustered around him like flies.

Midge stood looking after Gussie with a dumbfounded expression on her face.

"She called me a brat," she said finally, in a stunned voice. "And she was really nasty."

"I don't think she liked being called Gussie," I said.

"That's the only name I know," Midge said. "That's what her sister calls her. I was just trying to be friendly."

"She thinks she's a dignified young lady," I said. "If that is her boyfriend over there you're lucky he wasn't within hearing distance. She would have been even nastier."

"I guess she's gone high hat," Midge said. "Some reporter took her picture playing tennis a week or two ago and they published it in the paper. There was some caption about her being one of the lovely local tennis players gracing the Princeton courts. Phooey!"

The three girls were still talking to the young man. I would have thought he'd be tired of holding his bag of groceries but he didn't seem to mind. Gussie was all gay and animated now. She began bouncing one of her tennis balls on the pavement by the supermarket door.

"Look at her show off," Midge said. "So I'm a brat!" She was over being hurt and was getting annoyed. "So she's too stuck up to answer to the name of Gussie."

Herbert gave up nudging me to throw his ball and nudged Midge. She looked down at him and then over at Gussie. "Any cars moving anywhere near?" she asked.

"Don't see any."

Midge grabbed Herbert's ball and pretended to throw it straight at the supermarket door. "Fetch, Herbert!" she said.

Herbert started full tilt in the direction he thought Midge had thrown his ball. Somewhere between where we were standing and Gussie's group he must have spotted the tennis ball Gussie was bouncing up and down. Of course, he thought it was his.

Once he saw it, Herbert kept his eye on the ball. It was on an upward bounce as he got there and he went up in the air after it. He caught it but grazed the young man who was holding the groceries and slammed right into Gussie. The young man dropped his bag and Gussie tumbled backward right into a woman wheeling an overloaded cart. The cart went over, the woman went down, and Gussie went with her.

In the shock of hitting Gussie almost head on, Herbert lost the ball. It went rolling through the open door into the market. Herbert shot through the door after it like a flash. A whole bunch of people inside began yelling and screaming and pushing and running. The young man who had dropped his bag of groceries looked down at the mess in disbelief and then helped the fallen woman to her feet. Gussie managed to get up by herself. Something in the cart—probably a bottle of syrup or molasses—had broken, and she must have sat in it. The whole back of her white tennis shorts was soaked in something brown and sticky. The cart of spilled groceries had packages broken open and things like sugar and flour spilled all over and mixed with the sticky syrup.

The crowd around the spilled groceries grew larger and larger because no one could get in or out the doors. Then a boy who had been gathering carts in the parking lot came up pushing a huge row of carts, which added to the traffic jam. All the late arrivals in the crowd tried to peer over the shoulders of the people in front. In the middle of it all Herbert came trotting out. He jumped over all the mess and slipped through the crowd without any trouble. He had the tennis ball in his mouth. He looked around and saw Midge. He came trotting happily in our direction.

"I think we have enough interviews," Midge said. "Let's go."

We ducked between two parked cars. Herbert caught up with us a few seconds later, wagging his tail happily. He was proud of having retrieved that ball and I think he deserved to be.

"A place like this with so many cars isn't safe for Herbert," Midge said. "Maybe we ought to take him home."

We kept a row of cars between us and the supermarket and began walking toward the other end of the shopping center. A moment later I spotted Mrs. Glass driving in. We trotted up to the car, Herbert right beside us, still carrying his ball.

"Hi, Mom," Midge said. "Will you do us a favor and drive us over by Lily's house?"

"I guess so," Mrs. Glass said, "but I haven't time for you to visit with Lily. I have an appointment later this afternoon and I'm running late."

"Oh, I don't want to see Lily," Midge said. "We just want to take Herbert home. He lives down the street from Lily."

"All right. Hop in," Mrs. Glass said.

Midge got in front with her mother and Herbert and I got in back. As we drove away we could see the crowd by the supermarket door was even larger now.

"What is all that about?" Mrs. Glass asked.

"People get all excited over nothing," Midge said. "We saw it all. It wasn't anything much."

"Just what did happen?"

"Gussie and two other girls were talking to a boy outside the market. He was holding a bag of groceries and for some reason he dropped it. A woman coming out just then tripped and her cart of groceries went over and made a much bigger mess. In the middle of it all Gussie slipped and sat down in a puddle of syrup from a broken syrup bottle. She was wearing her white tennis shorts. It was a riot." Midge began to laugh.

"It's not a laughing matter," Mrs. Glass said. "She might have sat on some broken glass."

"No such luck," Midge said. "Anyhow, it serves her right. I said hello to her very politely and she bawled me out for calling her 'Gussie' and said I was a brat!"

"Hmm," Mrs. Glass said. "You didn't happen to bump into this boy with the groceries, did you?"

"Henry and I were forty feet away."

She sat up very straight and dignified but not for long. She began to giggle.

"Herbert made out pretty well," I said. "He has an almost new tennis ball."

"There is something a bit odd about this whole episode," Mrs. Glass said thoughtfully.

Mrs. Glass reminds me of my mother once in a while. They both seem to have something I read about that is called "extra-sensory perception" and they know about things without anyone actually telling them. I decided it was time to be real quiet and not even think about what had happened outside the supermarket. So I thought about ways to run a kite-flying contest all the way home.

Friday, August 23

It has been rainy and drizzly all day. I guess that is just as well, because Midge and I have spent the entire day working up a report on our poll. It would have been much worse sitting inside if it had been nice weather outside.

We got more than fifty answers to our questions. Figuring out different categories of allowances didn't take long. It was even fun. When we got through it was plain that Deirdre was being underpaid. At least it was plain to Midge and me. The problem was to convince her father. We had to write the report so that he would see that he was stingy. We finally decided that we would start off with a written page or so explaining how and when and where the poll was taken. Next we would show a table of our results. Finally we would give our conclusions. The conclusion was the rough part. We rewrote it at least six times. Midge copied the last draft very carefully since her handwriting is better than mine. This is how it read:

REED AND GLASS THINK TANK
Results of Poll Taken August 22
Concerning Kids' Allowances

This poll was taken in the Princeton area. More than seventy-five people were questioned. People who had no children between the ages of seven and fourteen were ruled out as their answers would not mean much in our study. Also grandparents' replies were not included as we found that they very often have inaccurate information about their grandchildren's allowances. The results were as follows:

Parents who give their children no allowance at all
                                                                                    3
Parents who give their children occasional money but
   no regular allowance   4
Parents who give their children a weekly allowance
   of 50 cents or less   4
Parents who give their children a weekly allowance
   of 50 cents to $1.00   13
Parents who give their children a weekly allowance
   of more than $1.00 but less than $2.00   27
Parents who give their children a weekly allowance
   of more than $2.00   11

Note: None of the above figures include lunch money
   for school days.

47

The answers to the questions concerning the effects of giving a child a regular weekly allowance were:

Do you think an allowance helps a child learn how to handle money sensibly?   Yes 51   No 6

Do you think allowing a child to buy some of his or her clothes or school supplies gives him or her valuable experience in how to shop?
                                        Yes 49   No 9

Do you think having an allowance much smaller than that of his or her peers may cause a child problems of adjustment? (Note: One person being interviewed stated that she thought a few problems were good for children.)   Yes 39   No 18
                                        No Opinion 8

Do you think a child's allowance should be adjusted now and then to keep up with inflation?
                                        Yes 38   No 16
                                        No Opinion 4

If a child is allowed to buy himself or herself an item such as a sweater, will he pay more or less for the item than he would have if he picked it out and you paid?   Less 41
                                        About the same 13
                                        More 4

The conclusion of the REED AND GLASS organization, drawn from these results, is that a child between the

48

ages of seven and fourteen should have a weekly allowance of about $1.50, not counting money for school lunches. A parent who provides his child with an allowance of this amount will encourage him to learn how to handle money wisely and how to shop and learn values. Too small an allowance can cause the child problems of adjustment unless he understands that the reason for his small allowance is that it is all the family can afford. If the parent can afford a normal allowance but refuses to give it, then he must be stingy.

I showed the report to Uncle Al just before dinner. He read it through very carefully.

"That's quite a report," he said. "Quite a report."

"Midge and I are worried that we don't say enough at the beginning and the end," I said. "But I don't know what else to say."

"Well, most reports are too longwinded anyhow. I think you have said everything necessary. What do you feel is wrong with it?"

"It doesn't sound very impressive."

"I think it is quite impressive," Uncle Al said. "I have read a lot of reports, a great many of them written by Princeton professors and other professors. I've discovered some common mistakes. If you haven't much to say, then use three times as many words as are necessary. And if you don't have anything really important to say, confuse everyone by replacing all the short words with long ones. Now you and Midge have avoided both of those faults."

"Then you think it is all right the way it is?"

"Well . . . I'd make a few changes," he said. "In the

heading of your report I'd change the word 'kids' to 'young people.' Sounds more dignified. Now that last sentence is quite clear, I admit. What you are saying in effect is that this man—what is his name?"

"Mullins."

"If this fellow Mullins doesn't raise his daughter's allowance then he is a stingy skinflint."

"That's right. The survey proves it."

"We won't argue that point," Uncle Al said. "Maybe he is. But it's a little strong and a bit blunt. This is one of those places where it is wise to use some of those big words we were talking about. And plenty of them. Your parents are in the diplomatic service, so you should know what I mean. Diplomats and politicians can use more words and say less than anyone. Let's express this point in their language. It might help."

"I've got a pencil. Okay."

"Let's change that last sentence to read 'If the parent can afford the prevailing allowance it is a wise investment which will be repaid in the enduring respect and affection of the child.' "

"That sounds great!" I said. "Anything else?"

"Well, this isn't too easy to read. Do you suppose you could get Midge to copy it over?"

"She did copy it over. That's her best handwriting. Mine is even worse."

Uncle Al nodded. "Well, I wouldn't say either of you would ever win many prizes in penmanship. And ruled yellow paper isn't so good either. Doesn't look professional."

"We have ordered some stationery with the name of our think tank printed on it," I said. "But it will be a week or maybe two before we get it. We'd like to get this report over to Mr. Mullins soon. If he does raise her allowance then she's losing money every week we delay."

"You have a point there," Uncle Al admitted. "Tell you what I'll do. I'll take this to the office tomorrow. I'll ask Miss Saunders to run this through the word processor and print out a couple of copies. I'll have her put your firm's name at the top and the title of the report just as you have it, except we will change that word 'kids.' Then in brackets I will have her put 'Advance copy—computer printout.' For some strange reason people are very impressed with computer printouts."

"That would be great," I said.

I've met Miss Saunders lots of times. She is Uncle Al's receptionist, telephone operator, stenographer, and assistant in his insurance business. She is tall and skinny and sour-looking, and always complaining about how she is overworked. However, if she would do our report, I wasn't going to object. I didn't think Midge would either.

Saturday, August 24

*Uncle Al took our report to the office this morning. Al-*though it is Saturday and Miss Saunders doesn't usually work on Saturdays, she came in to do something with a special insurance policy. She took our report and ran it through the computer, using a word-processing program. It looks like a million dollars. The computer justifies. That means that it spaces the words so they line up straight on both the left- and right-hand sides, like the pages of a book. Miss Saunders did a beautiful job, making the heading in real black type and underlining certain parts. She even put one copy in one of those limp fiber bindings. I guess Miss Saunders isn't really sour at all and Midge says that as soon as we get our stationery we will write her a nice letter of thanks.

We wanted to get the report to Deirdre Mullins right away. We called her but she said her bike had a flat tire and wouldn't be repaired until Monday. Midge and I are in bad shape for transportation these days. Last summer I used an old bike which Uncle Al used to ride for exercise years ago, but while I was away last winter it fell over as he was backing the car out and got wrecked. Midge left her bike out when they went away one weekend and it was stolen. So we have to depend on Mrs. Glass or Uncle Al to drive us if we have very far to go. Neither one had the time to drive us to Lawrenceville.

We were up at our office admiring our fancy report and talking about how to run a kite-flying contest when Mr. Shapiro drove in his driveway.

"Do you know what Mr. Shapiro has in his garage?" Midge asked.

"Snakes," I said. "Maybe a monster?"

"Not even near," Midge said. "He has a tandem bicycle. He said I could ride it if I wanted. But of course one person on a tandem bicycle doesn't make sense. With two people it would be fun. Want to try it?"

"Sure. We could ride over and deliver our report."

The tires were soft because the bike hadn't been used in a long time but Mr. Shapiro had a pump. We finally got the tires hard enough and started off. Riding a tandem bike is different from riding an ordinary bike but you soon get the hang of it. Midge sat in front steering, since she knew the way. There isn't much traffic on our road and it didn't matter that we wobbled and wavered around at first. By the time we got to the Princeton–Lawrenceville road, which is heavily traveled, we were doing fine.

With two people pedaling you can make very good time, and pedaling up a long hill is much easier than on a one-person bike. It's at least four miles from Grover's Corner to Deirdre's house, but we were there in no time at all. She lives in a beautiful stone house with a huge lawn stretching to a hedge by the side of the road. There was a nice swimming pool out back. Midge and I looked around and knew our report was right on target. Deirdre's father was giving her a pretty skimpy allowance.

Deirdre thought the report was great. Her father was going to be home later that afternoon, and she planned to give him the report as soon as he arrived. She invited us to take a swim, but neither of us had brought a bathing suit. It was hot enough that I would have jumped in wearing the old khaki shorts I had on. Midge was not interested. She was wearing a brand-new pair of pale blue shorts and a blue blouse. I guess they were very special, because she had been annoyed earlier when she appeared in them and I hadn't noticed. She did look very nice, but I don't think girls should expect boys to notice clothes. At least they shouldn't get mad if they don't.

"That front tire still looks a little soft," I said as we rode out.

"I have an idea," Midge said. "Since we didn't go swimming, let's go on into Princeton instead of going straight home. We can get the tire checked at a service station and then go get an ice-cream cone at that place on Nassau Street that has all different flavors and add-ons and blends.

We started pedaling toward Princeton. By this time we

felt like experts although it still seemed strange to be riding in back. You have handlebars but they don't mean anything.

We were moving along at a good clip when a pickup truck pulled up beside us. It was one of those fancy jobs with special springs to make the truck body higher than ordinary trucks. It had big broad tires, too. Two boys were in the truck. The one on the passenger side rolled down his window and stuck his head out.

"Why don't you get a horse, Midge?" he yelled.

"Get lost," Midge said and stuck her nose in the air.

The driver put on a burst of speed and the truck roared up the road.

"Friends of yours?" I asked.

"I know them from school," Midge said. "Dumb, both of them or they would have been out of school by now instead of only two years ahead of me. Kevin, he's the one driving, was three years in the eighth grade. The kids used to say he would be the first student in junior high ever to vote."

About a mile up the road we came to a nursery stand. It had all sorts of shrubs, plants, and trees for sale. The pickup truck was in the parking space in front. The two boys got in the cab as we approached.

"Slow down and let them go on ahead," Midge said.

They didn't drive away, however. The driver got out and looked at his left rear tire. Then he stood for a minute saying something to a boy who was watering some plants with a hose. By this time, even dawdling along, we were almost opposite them, so we picked up speed again.

The water that had spilled over from watering the plants had run down into the shallow gutter between the highway and the nursery parking lot. Midge moved over a tiny bit to the left to keep from riding through the muddy puddles. The driver of the truck hopped in and took off with a screech of tires just ahead of us. Those big flat tires went through a huge puddle, throwing up a sheet of muddy water that soaked Midge from the waist up. I was just far enough behind her that I got only a few drops.

I don't know if it was an accident or not, but they saw what had happened. The boy in the passenger seat leaned out and shouted something that we couldn't hear. We could see that he was laughing.

We had to stop. Not only had the muddy water spattered Midge's clothes and face, some had gone in her eyes so she couldn't see. We pulled over on the shoulder and got off the bike. Midge had one tissue in her pocket and I had a handkerchief that was reasonably clean.

"Look at my new clothes," she wailed. "They're ruined! Those miserable jerks! They did that on purpose."

I knew how she felt. Last summer I was walking down the road at Grover's Corner when one of the Sebastian twins ran through a puddle of mud in their little MG and splashed all over me.

"Let's go back to the nursery stand," I suggested. We were only a few yards away. "They have water and you can wash your face."

"Not me!" Midge said. "The reason they were there was to see JoJo Coletti, who works at the stand. He's a friend of theirs and he'll tell them how badly they soaked me. I'm not going to give them that satisfaction."

56

She got her face fairly dry with my handkerchief, but it was still streaky and dirty. We got back on the bike with me in front this time.

"Let's not go to Princeton," Midge said a minute later. "I look awful and I'll be sure to run into everyone I know."

"We're two-thirds of the way there," I protested. "We can turn off Nassau Street and take the back streets. You stay someplace out of sight and I'll go get the ice-cream cones."

That's what we did. When we got to Bank Street we turned left and went through Hullfish and Spring Streets to Van Deventer Street. We stopped beside the Garden Theater. Midge flatly refused to go back onto Nassau Street again. We leaned the bike against a tree. It was about half a block away from the ice-cream place.

I left her standing in the shade by the bike and hurried across the intersection. There was a short line at the ice-cream store so I was gone a few minutes. I got butter almond for me and rum raisin for Midge and got back just in time to see the two boys in the pickup truck park almost in front of Midge. The boy in the passenger seat hopped out and put money in the parking meter.

"Hi, Midge," he said. "Been making mud pies or something?"

"You fiend!" Midge said. "I expect you to pay the cleaning bill for these clothes. We almost had an accident, you splashed so much mud in my eyes."

The driver of the truck joined his friend on the sidewalk. He looked at Midge and said, "Who is this dirty little girl, Jim?"

They both laughed as though he had said the funniest

thing in the world and walked off. I handed the cup of
rum-raisin ice cream to Midge and for a minute I thought
she was going to run after them and throw it. But her
appetite won and she finally simmered down and began
eating her ice cream.

We were still eating when a young man hurried up to
a small car parked directly behind the pickup truck. He
looked at the meter and unlocked the door of his car.

"That's timing it," he said, nodding his head down the
street. "My meter has run out and here comes the law."

Way down the block there was a policeman in one of
those golf carts they use when checking parking meters.
As I watched he stopped beside a car and took out his
ticket book.

"Henry, our think tank has got a new customer," Midge
announced.

"Who?" I asked.

"Me. Our next project is how to get even with Jim
Bogden and Kevin Menzil. I wish they had forgotten to
put money in the meter. I'd go down and tell that policeman to hurry up and give them a ticket."

There's a slight hill as you go up Van Deventer Street
to Nassau. The parking space directly behind the pickup
truck was vacant where the Honda had stood and the
meter had expired.

"Simple," I said. "Just move the truck back one parking
space and you'll be all set." I took another big spoonful
of ice cream.

Midge's eyes widened. "Henry, you're right," she said.
"You are a genius! All you have to do is hop in, take

58

off the brake, and let the truck roll back."

"All *I* have to do!" I said. "You're the one who is getting even."

"But you know how to drive!" she said. "You are bigger and stronger and older than I am."

All of this was probably true. I did know how to drive a little but Midge probably did too. And I was still several years from getting a driver's license.

"I haven't got a driver's license," I pointed out.

"You wouldn't be driving—you'd be parking. In fact you'd just be changing the parking a little. Hurry or they'll come back or the policeman will get here."

"That's the trouble. They'll probably both get here just as I get in the truck."

"I'll keep watch," Midge said. "I'll go up to the corner of the theater where I can see down the street. If the policeman arrives, you are just sitting in the truck. Come on, don't let such a brilliant idea go to waste. Boys are supposed to be braver and more daring than girls."

"What happened to all that women's lib stuff?" I asked. "My mother warned me about scheming women."

I didn't like the idea but I headed toward the truck. Midge grabbed my cup of ice cream. "You'll need both hands," she said, and began running toward the corner.

I hurriedly climbed into the driver's seat. I looked in the rearview mirror and saw the policeman stop at another car and begin writing out a ticket. It was really easy. The truck was out of gear so all I had to do was take off the hand brake and let it roll back about twenty feet. Then I put the hand brake back on and climbed out as fast as I could. I was standing by our bike when Midge got back. She handed me what remained of my ice cream. I finished it in one gulp.

"Let's get out of here," I said.

"We can't leave now," Midge said. "I want to be sure the policeman gives them a ticket."

The policeman got back in his little traffic cart and headed in our direction.

"That meter! That meter!" Midge said, jumping up and down. She was pointing at the car behind the truck. "The red flag is coming up and we don't want to delay him with an extra car. You've got some change."

I hurried over and put a dime in the meter. I was just in time. Seconds later the policeman rode by, looking carefully at every meter. He passed me and stopped at the truck. He got out, went in front of the truck, pulled out his book of tickets, and began writing. Midge smiled happily. I strolled over to join her next to our bike.

The policeman was still writing his ticket when the two boys appeared around the corner. They didn't notice at first. I think Kevin, who had been driving, was a little puzzled. Maybe he had a feeling the truck was further from the corner than where he had parked it but it is very hard to remember exactly where you parked your car in a long row. One thing he wasn't in doubt about and that was that he was getting a parking ticket.

"Hey," he yelled and hurried toward the policeman. Then he said something that I didn't catch.

"Sorry," the policeman said. "The meter has expired."

"But I put money in the meter," Jim said. "We had

half an hour and we haven't been gone fifteen minutes."

"I have to believe the meter," the policeman said, continuing with his writing.

"Then the meter isn't working right," Jim said. "I put money in it! Look, officer, that girl standing by that bike over there watched me put money in just a few minutes ago. Didn't you, Midge?"

The police officer looked over at Midge.

"I didn't see him put anything in that meter, officer," she said very sweetly. "He's probably too cheap to put money in a parking meter if he thinks he can get away for nothing."

The officer finished writing the ticket and handed a copy to Kevin. We got on our bike and Midge smiled and waved goodbye to Kevin and Jim.

Midge was in front again, and instead of turning away from Nassau Street she headed right for it. She pulled over to the curb in front of the ice-cream place.

"If you are brave enough to move the truck, I'm brave enough to buy us another ice cream no matter how I look. What flavor do you want?"

Sunday, August 25

Today has been a very busy day. Usually nothing much happens in Grover's Corner on Sunday. People aren't rushing to or from work, so there aren't many cars on the road. Most businesses are closed, but the Reed and Glass Think Tank had a big day.

The first thing that happened was that we got our stationery. Mrs. Glass picked it up yesterday. The stationery is quite impressive. So far we haven't had any use for it, except for the letter of thanks we are going to write Miss Saunders. But it looks good in business to have your own stationery. Besides, as Midge pointed out, we will probably need some soon to send out bills for our services. Our stationery is printed in dark brown ink on cream-colored paper and the letterhead looks like this:

"Pretty fancy," Midge said. "Wait until I write my friend Jessica on this."

Agony came into the barn, so Midge held the paper down where he could see it. "There you are, Agony, right in the middle. Aren't you proud? You know, Henry, we should have made him vice president in charge of something."

"He can be in charge of security, since he's a watchdog," I said. "But we aren't going to have the stationery reprinted because of that. We haven't paid for this yet."

The stationery was expensive and Mrs. Glass had paid for it. We had just enough between us to repay her, but it would leave us both broke. We were deciding whether we should pay Mrs. Glass immediately or wait for a day or two when Deirdre rode up on her bike. She came bursting into the office with a big grin on her face.

"Wuk, wika warm, wuved wit," she said. Or at least that's what it sounded like.

"Gum," Midge said. She pointed at her mouth and then at her ear.

Deirdre took a huge wad of gum from her mouth and parked it behind her right ear again. Only this time she wasn't wearing her hair up in a bun and a big strand of hair got caught in the gum. She was too excited to notice.

63

"It worked. Worked like a charm!" she said. "It was brilliant, clever, original, well done, beautifully executed, and real cool! A great report!"

We thought so too but naturally Midge and I just smiled modestly.

"Did your dad like it?" I asked.

"He thought it was great. He said it was original thinking on my part to hire you two and that I had convinced him. He raised my allowance to three dollars. That's almost ten times what I was getting. And he gave me some back pay. So here's ten dollars as part payment. Have you got your bill ready yet?"

"Not quite," Midge said. "Our computer broke down."

"That report was written on a computer, wasn't it?" Deirdre asked. She looked carefully around the barn. "Where do you keep it?"

"We haven't really got one," Midge said. "Henry's Uncle Al had that run off for us. But we haven't totted up our time yet." Midge had a faraway look in her eye and I knew she was trying to figure out what would be a reasonable charge for Deirdre.

Deirdre spotted our stationery. Midge had left a sheet of it out on the table so it would have been hard not to see it.

"You've got your own stationery," she said, pulling it over to look at it. "That's nice, I like it." She looked at Midge. "You're Secretary and Treasurer?"

"I am."

"Isn't it a lot of work?"

"Well, yes, it is," Midge said with a wave of her hand.

"But I manage. Each of us has his or her own field. Henry does the real deep thinking and takes care of transportation questions—like parking cars and things like that. I take care of the money." She put the ten dollars that Deirdre had given her in her pocket. I made a note of it.

"Who is this Mr. Ony?" Deirdre asked. "Have I seen him?"

I looked over to where Agony had been sleeping. He was gone, probably outside looking for a squirrel or rabbit. "You may have seen him," I said. "He's around off and on."

"That's a funny name—Ony," Deirdre said.

"Probably Hungarian," Midge said. "He's the hairy type, but very smart."

I can never understand how someone who laughs as easily as Midge can look so serious when she is kidding. I had to get up and go look out the window.

"What does he do?"

"Special jobs," I said. "He's more of a consultant than a regular member of the firm."

"Then maybe you could use me after all."

"What do you mean?" I asked.

"I'd like to join your firm," Deirdre said. "I could help Midge. Be her assistant."

"That's not a bad idea," Midge said. "But right now we are working on only one job. What do you know about kite-flying contests?"

"Not much."

"That's about what we know," I said. "See what you can find out about them. If you can come up with some good ideas we will let you join the firm as a junior partner."

"I'll try," Deirdre said happily. "Where did you two get that wonderful bike?"

"We borrowed it from Mr. Shapiro down the street. He lets me borrow it any time but most of the time I haven't anyone to ride with me."

"I'll ride with you any time," Deirdre said. "I'll bet it's fun."

"It is when you aren't sitting in front when some car goes through a mud puddle just ahead of you. Tell you what, I'll go borrow it and we will ride part of the way home with you. You can ride on the tandem and one of us will ride your bike. Then we can switch, and you can go on home and we'll come back."

The idea appealed to everyone, so we went to get the bike. There was a short delay because Deirdre's hair was all tangled up in her gum. Midge had to cut away some hanks of hair. I thought Deirdre would throw away the gum but she didn't. She simply cut away the hairiest parts of it and popped the rest of it back in her mouth.

Midge rode the single bike and Deirdre rode on the tandem with me. She knew some back roads that I'd never been on before. We were pedaling along, enjoying the scenery, when we passed a small yellow bungalow. No one seemed to be around, but you could hear someone yelling in back of the house.

"That's where the Shultz twins live," Deirdre said. "They are friends of mine." I understood most of what she said. I guess cutting away some of her gum helped.

We were already past the house when Deirdre said, "Let's go back. The twins have a problem which would be just right for your think tank."

"What kind of problem?" I asked.

"Let them tell you," Deirdre said. "It will only take a minute. Believe me, they need help!"

We weren't in any hurry, so we turned around.

"Their father is dead," Deirdre explained on the way back. "Was killed in an automobile accident three or four years ago. Their mother works at the Educational Testing Service."

The twins were in the backyard. Willy, the boy, was pushing his sister, Betsy, in a swing. The swing was a single rope with a rubber tire on the bottom, tied to a limb way up in a very tall tree. It looked like a great swing. It seemed Willy was pushing Betsy too high, which was what the yelling was about. They quit when they saw us.

They certainly didn't look like brother and sister, much less twins. She was much smaller than he was. She had dark brown eyes, straight black hair, and a rather narrow face. She looked Spanish to me, while he looked just as you would expect a Wilhelm Shultz to look. He was blond, with a round chubby face and blue eyes. I suppose they were two years or so younger than Midge and me.

Deirdre took the gum out of her mouth while she explained who we were. "They're the Think Tank people," she said to the twins. "They just did a wonderful job for me. Got me a much bigger allowance. They think and then they come up with marvelous ideas. I thought maybe they could help you with your problem."

Willy gave a great sigh and his shoulders drooped. Betsy shook her head sadly and said, "You should have seen what we had for lunch. What a revolting mixture! What all was in it, Willy?"

"It makes me sick to my stomach just to think of it," Willy said. "Of course, I ate it, because there was nothing else and I was starving."

"What was it?" Midge asked.

"An awful hodgepodge of yogurt, alfalfa sprouts, and whole-grain-nut-and-dried-fruit mixture. It looked terrible, so I closed my eyes when I ate it. That made Mom mad." Willy gave another big sigh. "Meals used to be fun. I used to like to eat. But not now!"

It didn't look as though it had been so long ago that he had enjoyed eating, because he was still chubby. He wasn't really fat like Rodney, but he wasn't wasting away, either.

"Why does your mother feed you this gunk when you hate it so?" I asked.

"All mothers force their children to eat things they don't like," Deirdre said. "But the twins' case is so bad they might starve."

"My mom is on a health-food kick," Willy said glumly. "We have nothing in the house that isn't stuffed with all sorts of vitamins and extra nourishment. We've got special fortified juices, roughage, and dozens of special health foods. If it was as healthy as Mom claims I would be nine feet tall. And Betsy wouldn't be so sickly."

I looked at Betsy. She was skinny compared to her brother, but there didn't seem to be much wrong with her.

I guess Midge felt the same way because she asked, "What's wrong with Betsy?"

"Well, I had a bad cold last March," Betsy said, looking mournful. "And then in May I was laid up for two weeks."

"What with?"

"Sprained ankle."

"You can't really blame that on the food," Midge pointed out.

"Who knows," Willy said, looking very serious. "Maybe all this gunk she had to eat weakened her ankles."

"What the problem boils down to is that you don't like the food your mother is giving you. Is that right?" I asked.

"Well, yes," Willy admitted. "But like Deirdre said, it isn't the usual case of not liking *some* things she gives us. A year or so ago Betsy had to eat tapioca pudding once in a while even though she doesn't like it. And I had to eat cauliflower when we had it and I hate cauliflower. But most of the time the food we got was good. My mom is a good cook. But now we never get anything decent! We eat whole grains, sprinkle things with wheat germ, raw vegetables, yogurt, and sprouts, and all sorts of strange things like kasha, bulgur, buckwheat groats, and pilaf. We never go out anymore and eat real honest American foods like cheeseburgers and French fries and a chocolate milk shake, or a pizza, or a hot dog. You'd think we lived in a foreign country. We never get any meat any more. For a long while we got nothing but liver. Then it was chicken. I've got nothing against either but now and then I'd like to have a steak, or a pork chop, or some ham."

"And it's going to get worse," Betsy predicted. "Mom

is reading a book now about something called a 'macro-biotic' diet. I sneaked a look at it and from what I saw we're going to be eating nothing but brown rice. We never go to a supermarket anymore—just the health-food store. When we went to the supermarket we could slip a box of cookies into the cart now and then."

"Or a bag of potato chips," Willy said wistfully.

"Now nothing," Betsy said. "I'm almost looking forward to going back to school and eating those awful lunches they give us."

"You are really desperate when you look forward to school lunches," Midge said sympathetically. "Henry, I think they've got a real problem."

"You ought to see the cupboards in our kitchen," Willy said. "They would make you cry."

"Is your mother home?" Midge asked.

"No, she said she'd be gone an hour or so," Betsy said. "We didn't want to go with her because she is going to a new health-food store. Come on in and we'll show you."

The kitchen cabinets were exactly what Willy said. There was soybean flour, buckwheat groats, lentils, whole and cracked grains, and all sorts of terrible-sounding mixtures. I didn't see anything you could eat in an emergency—like a pretzel, or a potato chip, or a cookie.

"I can remember when we used to have wonderful breakfasts," Willy said mournfully. "Pancakes or waffles with maple syrup, scrambled eggs and bacon or sausage. Or when we were in a hurry, cereal with a banana and milk and sugar. Now we get that whole-grain gunk up there boiled up in a sort of soup with molasses to make it a little sweet. No white sugar at all!"

I looked at another shelf and saw some hominy grits, brown rice, split peas, and buckwheat flour. Even the tea was some special blend of herbs and spices.

"I'm hungry," Willy said. "I guess I'll have a piece of turnip. That's all there is. Want some?"

We said no and all went outside.

"There's no doubt about it. You have a problem," I said. "We'll think about it and come up with something."

"We have a package of something called 'blue-green manna,' " Betsy said. "The package claims it's the best brain food in the world. Willy ate almost a whole package and didn't come up with a single idea."

We rode off, but stopped when we were well out of sight to talk a minute. We were turning left at the next corner to go back home while Deirdre was going on toward her house. She took her wad of gum out and parked it on the handlebars of her bike.

"I really feel sorry for them," she said. "Do you suppose if you took a poll about what most parents feed their children it would help?"

"I doubt it," Midge said. "She must know that she isn't feeding them what normal mothers feed their kids. She believes all that stuff will make them extra healthy."

Monday, August 26

We had a conference of our entire staff this morning. Agony usually follows me everywhere I go, so both of us were down at the barn when Midge appeared about nine o'clock. She put Agony in a chair and moved him up to the conference table. Our conference table isn't one of those big shiny tables you see in most conference rooms. It's the same table that we use for our desk, and it's been used for lots of other things, too. Mrs. Glass used to keep house plants on it on their back porch and it has all sorts of stains all over it. It doesn't matter if Agony licks it now and then which he does if there are any crumbs lying around. We have cookies or snacks like potato chips now and then to keep up our energy. Thinking is very hard work.

"This Mrs. Shultz must not have any taste buds," I said to Midge. "She eats all this awful health food too. She must be real weird. Have you got any idea what she's like?"

Midge nodded. "I've seen her several times. She's about thirty, dark hair, nice smile, and very pretty. She looks normal enough. But you know how it is. Some people just don't care much for food. I knew a girl once who liked peanut-butter-and-sardine sandwiches. There are all sorts of freaks in this world."

"Then you don't think that if the twins persuaded her to go to a doctor for an examination he would find anything wrong with her taste buds? That they had withered away or something?"

"No. I'll bet that all taste buds look alike. We need a better idea than that."

"Well, maybe what we need is something that will make her revolted by this health-food gunk. I was thinking about it last night and I had several ideas that might work."

"All right," Midge said. "Let me get our pad and pencil."

"I think you can buy stuff, a liquid or a powder, that smells just awful," I said. "A few days ago Uncle Al got a letter from a fire-insurance company. It smelled like burning wood. What we need is something that smells like rotten eggs, or maybe a dead skunk. We could pour a little bit of it in all those canisters. When she opened any of them to use some of the groats or whatever, she would be so disgusted that she might go back to ordinary food."

Midge made some notes on her pad. "The general idea is good, but it is too dangerous to use."

"Why?"

"Well, nobody is going to eat a letter he gets in the mail, so it wouldn't make any difference if the stuff they put on it was poisonous. But you're talking about putting awful-smelling stuff on food. Suppose Mrs. Shultz has a bad cold and can't smell anything. She gets out some food and makes the twins eat it because it smells all right to her. The twins might end up in the hospital with food poisoning."

I had to admit that she had a point there. We talked over several other ideas which weren't much good either, and then Midge got what was left of a bag of potato chips we had opened the day before. We each got a handful and she gave the little broken pieces in the bottom of the bag to Agony. He ate them very politely. There were only two or three small crumbs left when two ants appeared. Agony watched them carefully for a few minutes and then he put his front feet on the edge of the table, stuck out that long tongue of his, and licked up the crumbs and the ants in one big lick. Then he curled up on the seat of his chair and went to sleep.

"I think he ate those ants," Midge said. "Ugh!"

"Maybe they're good," I said. "Monkeys eat lice that they pick off each other. I think little bugs are full of protein."

Midge gave a shudder. "I'd rather be undernourished."

"Agony may have a good idea," I said. "Most people get the shudders at the idea of eating bugs. Suppose we put bugs in those canisters of health foods? She'd probably throw the food out. If that happened several times she might think most health food had bugs and go back to honest-to-goodness food."

"Could be. It's the best idea so far. But some people aren't bothered much by bugs. I was over to a friend's house for breakfast one time. Her mother cooked oatmeal and it was full of cereal bugs. She said there were often cereal bugs in things like flour and oatmeal, especially in the summer. She poured water on the oatmeal and most of the bugs floated to the top. She just skimmed them off. I didn't eat much of that oatmeal because she didn't get nearly all the bugs! Ugh!"

"Well, bugs wouldn't poison anyone," I pointed out. "Or maybe a mouse would be better."

"Do you mean dead or alive?" Midge asked.

We decided it would be best to go have a conference with the twins. The tandem bike was still at Midge's house, as Mr. Shapiro had told her to keep it as long as she liked. We had gone part of the way to the twins' house when I noticed Agony tagging along behind us. He often goes with me on long hikes and he's very good at staying well over on the shoulder of the road. Since we were taking back roads we decided to let him come along.

"He's vice president of security," Midge said, "and he has come along to protect us."

We arrived at the Shultz house without any problem. It was about ten o'clock and a bulldozer next door was busy bulldozing. The operator was a man of thirty or so. He was tanned and husky-looking and had muscles in his upper arms that looked as though he could push the bulldozer around by himself. Another man, who seemed to be the helper, was loading some extra dirt into a small dump truck using a tractor with a front-end loader. A small reddish dog with a bushy tail was running around the site as though he was in charge. As soon as Agony saw the other dog, he ran over to greet him. They sniffed noses, bristled at each other and then went scampering across the bare ground right in front of the bulldozer. I went running after Agony, yelling at the top of my voice. I figured both dogs were about to be bulldozed out of this world.

The operator saw them. He not only lifted his blade in a second, he stopped that big machine in about two feet. He got down from his machine and was chasing the dogs from in front of the blade when I arrived.

"Jimmy, you take your friend and go play someplace else," he said to the little reddish dog.

"Agony, come here!" I yelled as I got there.

"That your beagle?" he asked.

"Yes. I'm sorry that he got in the way. I'll catch him and tie him up."

"Don't bother," he said. He was very friendly. "Jimmy is usually very good at staying clear of the machinery. They'll be all right. Let them play. I'll keep an eye out."

"What kind of dog is Jimmy?" I asked.

"Mongrel. But he's a bright little fellow."

The dogs ran off toward the rear of the lot, well away from where he was working, so the man climbed back on his machine. I stood for several minutes watching him and the dogs. He was a real artist with that bulldozer. He pushed and pulled on all sorts of levers and made it do everything but talk.

In the meantime Midge had found the twins. All three appeared from the woods at the back of the lot so I went to join them. In spite of all the noise that the bulldozer was making, Willy insisted on going in back of the garage to have our conference.

"Mom is home," he explained. "We don't want her to hear what we are saying."

"She sick?" Midge asked.

"No. She works at home a lot. She has a word processor and she does reports and all sorts of things on it."

"She arranged to stay home a lot a couple of years ago when we were smaller," Betsy added. "That way we didn't have to have a baby-sitter all the time or go away to some camp in the summer."

"That's nice," Midge said.

"It was nice," Betsy said sadly. "But now that she's on this health-food kick it means we get gunk for lunch too."

The bulldozer stopped and there was sudden quiet. "Someone building a house next door?" I asked.

"Yeah. I don't know who," Willy said. "I hope they have kids our age. Then we could be friends and maybe they would invite us over for a meal now and then."

"He's really good with that machine," I said. It had started again.

"He's good with the backhoe too," Willy said. "I watch him a lot, but never around noontime."

"Why not?" Midge asked.

"They eat right here on the job," Willy said sadly. "Every

day he sends his helper out in the pickup truck, and he brings back loads of food. They eat two or three hamburgers or steak sandwiches apiece. They have pizza some days. And milk shakes or sodas and then some cake or cookies. And they eat it right in front of you! It's inhuman."

"I think the bulldozer man is very handsome," Betsy said. "And he's friendly. His name is Don. I like him."

We finally got down to business. It wasn't too encouraging at first. The twins said their mother wasn't upset easily. Mice didn't bother her much at all. Now and then they would have one in the house and Mrs. Shultz would set a trap and catch it. She didn't like bugs, but they didn't make her shudder or shiver or scream.

"If she found bugs in one of those grain containers I think she'd just throw it out," Willy said.

"Or take it back to the store where she got it if it happened several times," Betsy said. "My mom doesn't let people push her around."

Midge was discouraged. "Well, I guess we cross that idea off."

"Isn't there anything that bothers her?" I asked. "Snakes, moldy food, wasps?"

"Spiders!" Betsy said suddenly. "Big spiders. She gets the screaming meemies when she sees a big spider. A long time ago an uncle or some relative was bitten by a spider and died. Mom was just a tiny girl but she remembered it. She has been scared to death of spiders ever since."

"I think it was a black widow spider," Willy said. "But it doesn't much matter. She practically has a fit over any spider. I think that is a great idea. We could catch some spiders and put one in every canister or package."

"We have to be careful," I warned. "We'd better do some research first and make certain we don't put any poisonous spiders in your food. We should get a book about spiders."

"I've got a much better idea," Midge said. "I know where we can get some fake spiders. I think they are made of rubber. Anyhow, they're not poisonous, and if they are in a tight container a long time they won't die and shrivel up."

Midge didn't say where she planned to get these fake spiders, so we talked a while longer and left. We promised to bring the spiders the next day.

As we got on our bike the young man who had been operating the front-end loader came over.

"Don said you wanted a few scoops of soil in that low spot," he said, waving his hand toward an area between the driveway and the edge of the lot.

"Yeah, water collects there every time it rains," Willy said. "I'll show you where I mean."

"I can see where it's low," the man said. "You'll want top soil there so you can get a decent stand of grass. I may have a scoop or two in the morning. I'll level it out with the edge of my scoop, but you'll have to do some hand raking. If I don't bring you enough in the morning we'll have more later when we do the final grading next door."

We said goodbye to the twins, called Agony, and rode off. When we were some distance down the road I said to Midge, "Where are you going to get the spiders?"

"Quakerbridge Mall," she said. "There's a place that has all sorts of imitation things—snakes, lizards, and the cutest little mice. They had dozens of spiders the last time I was there."

"Why were you being so mysterious about them?"

"I wasn't being mysterious. I was just protecting our trade secrets. If they knew where to get spiders why would they need our think tank?"

Tuesday, August 27

We got our spiders and we used them. The whole operation turned out to be a waste of time. Midge claims it was a disaster. It wasn't really that bad, but it would have been best if we hadn't protected our trade secrets quite so well. If the twins had bought their own spiders we wouldn't have lost anything except our time. As it is, we had a financial setback. The spiders cost $3.75. We used only one and it got us nowhere. So we not only won't get paid for our efforts, we now have three dollars' worth of unused spiders and not much chance of ever using them. Maybe we can trade them in on something like a mouse.

Midge got the spiders yesterday. They were very realistic, and certainly looked as though they would do the job. We were going to take them to the Shultz place early this morning, but it got cloudy about eight-thirty and by ten there was a violent thunderstorm. It thundered, there was lightning, and the rain came down in torrents. There were big puddles of water everywhere.

By lunchtime the roads had dried a little and we felt it was safe to ride over to the Shultzes'. We arrived about one-thirty or so and found the twins were inside. The thunder shower must have lasted longer there because the grass was still wet and a big puddle of water was standing beside the driveway in the spot that Willy and the young man from the construction job had discussed the day before. He had dumped one or two scoopfuls of dirt and had spread it out. It wasn't enough, and at least an inch of water was standing on top of the fresh dirt. That made a nice gooey mud puddle and of course Agony ran right through the middle of it on his way to join his new friend Jimmy.

We held our conference in back of the garage again.

"We bring spiders," Midge said proudly, opening the little box with the five spiders.

"They look great!" Willy said. "They'll scare the daylights out of Mom."

"We planned to get them over here in time for you to put them in something you would get for lunch," I said. "But it rained."

"We could put them in that bran mixture," Betsy said. "We had an awful concoction for lunch and both of us complained. Mom promised she would make us some cookies as soon as she finished the report she's working on. And she's almost done."

"Put a spider in the flour and that mixture of nuts, raisins, and grains. She'll use one or the other," Willy said. "And maybe we should put some in some breakfast foods."

"A spider a day keeps the health food away," Midge said, and began laughing. Midge is not very modest about laughing at her own jokes.

"We better get going," Betsy said.

They took three spiders and disappeared into the house. They were gone only a minute or two.

"All set," Betsy said when they reappeared. "And Mom is on the last page of her report."

We decided to wait a few minutes to see what, if anything, happened. While we were waiting we tried the twins' swing, which was just as great as it looked. I got in first and Willy pushed me. The tire kept spinning as it swung, which made me a little dizzy, but it was fun.

We had been playing about fifteen minutes, and Midge was in the swing, when she began pointing and yelling something about Agony. I stopped the swing to find out what she was saying.

"Agony and that dog," she said. "They're digging a big hole in the flowerbed. You better stop them."

I looked, and sure enough Agony and Jimmy were digging like mad in the flowerbed right beside the back steps. They were probably after a field mouse or a mole.

There was a piercing shriek from inside the house and Mrs. Schultz came bursting out. She went down the back steps so fast I'm not sure she really touched them. When she got on the grass a few feet away she stopped, took a deep breath, and shook her head. I guess she figured she had escaped from the spider and was feeling a little embarrassed about screaming so loudly. The bulldozer operator had shut off his machine near the edge of the lot and was looking at something in the engine. He looked up to see what was the matter.

Just then Mrs. Shultz noticed the two dogs digging in her flowers. She was already excited and this made her furious. Later I saw what a big hole they had made and I suppose she had a right to be annoyed.

"Get out of that garden!" she shouted.

The dogs paid no attention. A bundle of newspapers, all carefully tied, had been placed on the top step ready to go to the recycling center. Mrs. Shultz was so mad she picked it up and threw it at the two dogs. It was heavier than she expected and her aim was no good. It hit a tall plant with pink flowers and flattened it. The string came undone and the papers scattered all over.

"Uh-oh," Willy said. "I should have taken that bundle to the garage. What a mess."

"That was a pink aster she got somewhere," Betsy said. "Now she'll really be mad."

She was! She grabbed a paper, rolled it, and started toward the dogs. They left the flowerbed and ran toward the driveway. I don't think they knew they were in danger; they were still after that mouse. Mrs. Shultz was right behind them. At the far edge of the drive, the mouse must have reversed course and so did Jimmy. Agony was a little slower to realize what had happened and he went on into the muddy puddle on the other side. Jimmy ran directly into Mrs. Shultz. She stumbled, took two or three steps trying to regain her balance, and then fell flat on her face in the middle of the puddle, right where the fresh dirt had been dumped. She splashed muddy water all over Agony. He sat down in the middle of the puddle and gave her a surprised look.

The bulldozer operator watched it all. He stepped across the edge of the lot, walked into the middle of the puddle, and picked up Mrs. Shultz as though she were a rag doll. He carried her over to where it was dry and set her down on her feet. She was a mess! Her face was covered with mud, and what had been a pale yellow dress was soaked with muddy water and was dripping all over the place. Even her hair was soaked, and straggled down over her forehead in a stringy mess.

She spat some muddy water out of her mouth, wiped her lips with a muddy hand, and managed to gasp, "Was that your dog?"

"I'm afraid one of them was," he said politely. "I'm sorry."

"Sorry!" she said in a furious voice. She looked down at herself. "Look at me!" she wailed. "Get off my property and take that dog of yours with you."

She turned and ran into the house. Willy and Betsy looked after her, completely speechless. I guess they had never seen her so mad.

"Quick!" I said. "Go get that spider. If she finds it and discovers it's a fake, we're in real trouble."

Willy scurried for the house with Betsy right behind him. I went to the garage and got a rake and a shovel. I filled in the hole the dogs had dug while Midge gathered up the newspapers. There wasn't much we could do about the pink aster. It had been flattened for this year, so we didn't touch it. Willy and Betsy came out as we were finishing.

"She dropped the canister and spilled that stuff all over the floor," Willy said. "Betsy swept it up. I stepped on the spider and then flushed it down the toilet."

That seemed a pretty drastic thing to do with a 75-cent rubber spider, but at least he could truthfully tell his mother he had taken care of the spider. He gave me back all the others.

Midge looked at her watch. "I think it is about time we went home, Henry," she said. "I have some work I have to do."

That seemed like a wise idea. I whistled to Agony, who came right away. I think he knew something was wrong. I could hear water running somewhere in the house. I suppose Mrs. Shultz was taking a shower. It seemed a good time to leave. The twins walked down to the edge of the road with us.

"What will we do now?" Willy asked sadly. "Give up?"

I was about to say yes when Midge said, "We have a long-range plan that we are working on."

I said nothing, and we pedaled away. When we were halfway home I said, "Well, that was a good idea. It just didn't work out right. How could we have known there would be a mud puddle right there or that the dogs would dig in her garden?"

"You win some, you lose some," Midge said. "Was she a mess!"

"What long-range plan do you have?" I asked.

"Before you know it they'll be through school and going to college," Midge said. "Then they can eat anything they want."

That seemed very long range to me.

Wednesday, August 28

I felt out of sorts all morning. It was hot and steamy even though the sun was hidden behind a blanket of clouds. I like New Jersey, and Uncle Al claims the Princeton area is the best part of the state. But the climate is awful a good part of the time. I also felt miserable about how our plan had worked yesterday. I suppose I should say the way our plan hadn't worked. Running a business has its headaches, even a simple business like a think tank.

I went down to the barn and began reading a good adventure story about two boys who were hunting a lost Incan treasure in the Andes, and I had almost forgotten about our big flop yesterday when Midge appeared.

"Hi," she said. "Business doesn't seem exactly rushing, does it?"

"It's awful," I said. "And it will get worse if people hear about that mess yesterday."

"I've quit worrying about yesterday. We'll come up with another idea that will work."

"Except it won't be safe to show up around the Shultz house. Mrs. Shultz was really boiling. And don't forget one of the dogs who dug up her garden is a member of our firm."

"True, but she doesn't know that," Midge said. "I talked to Mom about the Shultz case this morning. She pointed out that a diet like that isn't easy on the mother either. You can't just run over to the nearest supermarket and get the things you want. You have to go to special stores and read all the labels carefully. A cousin of mine once stayed with us for several weeks. She was allergic to almost all normal foods. My mother went crazy trying to buy food for her."

"So?" I asked. I didn't get the point.

"Well, Mrs. Shultz will get tired of all this special shopping after a while. When she does she'll start buying food again at the supermarket and the twins will get a halfway normal diet."

"That's not much to tell them," I said gloomily. "And I don't think the twins will pay us much if we just say someday things will get better. They want the problem solved now."

"Well, the other thing my mom said was that Mrs. Shultz probably needed something important to think about to get her mind off the health-food bit."

That sounded as though it might have more possibilities.

"Maybe we could think up some big problem for her—a real crisis."

"Maybe we could find a half dozen or so really big dogs to all dig at once in her garden," Midge said. "That would be a real crisis."

Neither of us really liked that idea. We discussed several other ideas like a big explosion in the kitchen which would spoil all the health food or a leak in the kitchen roof that would do the same thing. The trouble with ideas like those is that they would cause real damage. Then we talked about having one of the twins pretend to be so sick that he or she would have to be taken to the hospital.

"Hospital food is even worse than health food," Midge said. "Also, going to a hospital is expensive and we probably wouldn't fool a smart doctor very long anyhow. I guess we are stumped, Henry. Our think tank has thunk and thunk and got nowhere."

"There's no such word as thunk," I said.

"There ought to be," Midge said. "To rhyme with flunk, which is what we did on this case."

Just then, a car pulled off the road sort of half into the remains of the old driveway which went by the barn to the house, back when there was a house. A woman was driving. She turned off the motor and got out. She walked to the rear of her car and looked down at the left rear wheel. Midge got up and went to the window.

"Flat tire," she said. "Gee, it's been a long time since I saw anyone with a flat tire."

We went outside to see if we could be of any help. The woman saw us.

"Do you know where there is a telephone I could use?" she asked. "I guess I had best call a garage. I don't want to change a tire in this dress and I am not certain I even know how. I don't know where the jack is or how it works."

"You could use our telephone," Midge offered, nodding toward her house. "But there isn't anyone closer than Princeton, and it takes a long time to get anyone to come. Lots of places won't come at all."

"I know," the woman said with a sigh. "I suppose I could call my husband and see if he has any suggestions. The trouble is that he will feel he ought to come himself. I hate bothering him at work."

"I think I could change it," I said.

"That would be wonderful if you could," she said.

I found the jack in the trunk. It had never been used. It took several minutes to figure out where it went and how it worked, but Midge got out the instruction book and it had pictures. We got the wheel jacked up and after some hard yanking we got the nuts loose. From there on it was easy. The woman didn't do much, but then she was wearing a fancy white dress. Midge was a big help, though. I'll bet she could change a tire by herself almost as fast as I could.

"You two are the Reed and Glass of the sign up there?" the woman asked.

"He's Henry Reed and I'm Midge Glass," Midge said, handing me the next nut to put on.

"And you have a think tank?"

Midge nodded yes.

"What sort of work does your think tank do?"

"We handle all sorts of problems," Midge said airily. "Not deep scientific projects but practical ones. We just did a job for a girl who felt her allowance was too small. We took a poll, drew up a report, and proved to her father that she deserved more."

"That sounds like a thoroughly practical problem and solution," the woman admitted. "I have an uncle who is with a very prestigious institute out in California. I understand it is considered an outstanding think tank, but I have never understood one thing he has ever done. No doubt he has a great mind, but he can't boil water without burning it."

I put the hubcap back on and the flat tire back in the trunk. "There's not much use fastening that down," I told her. "They will have to take it out to fix it anyhow."

"Quite right," she said. "I can't tell you how appreciative I am." She opened her purse and took out a five-dollar bill and handed it to me. "I want you two to take this."

"We didn't change your tire to earn money," I said. "Just to help you out."

"I know, but think of what it would have cost me if I had got someone out from Princeton."

I protested again but not too hard. I took the five-dollar bill and gave it to Midge. "We'll put it in the firm's treasury. Thank you."

The woman started to get back in her car and then paused. "Are you two the entire firm?"

"Us and Henry's dog," Midge said with a grin. "He's on our letterhead too."

"I'm sure he appreciates that," the woman said with a smile. "You know I might just have some work for your think tank. I have a problem and it needs a practical, tactful solution."

"That's our specialty," Midge said. "Henry's father is in the diplomatic service, so Henry's diplomatic. I'm practical."

"What is your problem?" I asked.

"Geese," she said. "Canada geese. Too many of them."

"They're good eating," Midge said. "Why wouldn't that solve your problem? Have a big goose cookout."

"That's what my husband threatens to do. He says he is going out with a gun some morning and shoot enough geese to fill the freezer. But there are several things wrong with that. One—he doesn't have a gun and his eyesight is so poor he wouldn't hit anything anyhow. And second, the geese aren't on our place most of the time—they are next door. By the way, I'm Mrs. Walcott. Are you familiar with the roads around here?"

"I am," Midge said. "I have always lived around here. Henry is just here for his third summer."

"Well, if you go down Cold Soil Road and take a right on Seton Brook Lane we are the fourth house in. Do you know about where that is?"

Midge nodded. "I think so."

"Anyhow, an elderly woman lives next door. She has about ten acres. She is a dear person and we are very good friends. She does everything she can to protect wildlife—I think she has at least twenty bird feeders, which she keeps filled year round. Also, she has a small pond,

93

which is near the edge of her property. Actually, it is much nearer our house than hers. It's lovely. We can sit at our dinner table and look out at the water. At least, it was lovely for several years, but now the place is completely overrun with Canada geese."

"Any particular reason why there are so many?" I asked.

"Just that they multiply and they have few natural enemies anymore. No one feeds them, I can assure you of that. About four years ago, when the first pair made their nest there, we were delighted. They hatched out six goslings, which were darling. We watched them grow up. The next year there were four pairs nesting. This year there were eleven pairs, with an average of about four goslings each. With the parents that makes over fifty geese."

"Do they fly south in the winter?" I asked.

"They do not!" Mrs. Walcott said. "The Canada geese around here do not migrate anymore. They have a very soft life right here and see no reason to leave."

"Why don't you want them on the pond next door?" I asked. "Aren't they fun to watch?"

"They are beautiful to watch," Mrs. Walcott agreed. "Especially when they glide down from the sky and land on the pond. If we just had an occasional visit, even from a large flock, I wouldn't mind. But these geese that we have now are permanent. I suppose most of them were born there. They think it is their pond."

"What do they do that you don't like?" Midge insisted.

"I could write a book about it," Mrs. Walcott said wearily. "First, beginning in early April, a hundred or so fly in and begin fighting over nesting sites. They honk and squawk and make an incredible noise, starting about four o'clock in the morning. It is absolutely impossible to sleep. Geese may be companionable birds who like to live in large flocks, but they are certainly not always peaceful. They have terrible fights. They even try to drown each other. If another goose gets near a nest that is not its own, the owners drive it away with honks and hisses and screams. They do the same thing if anything comes near their goslings. For almost three months there is pandemonium on that pond—constant fighting and noise. But that is only part of it.

"Geese are vegetarians; they eat grass and weeds, largely. My husband is very proud of his lawn. He keeps it cut and trimmed neatly. The geese think it is all just for them. They don't like the old, tough grass in the pasture surrounding their pond; they prefer our lawn with its nice tender grass. When you have fifty geese or more spending the entire day on your lawn, it can get pretty messy. You wouldn't dare sit down on that beautiful grass. I used to take a blanket out in warm weather and take a sunbath. Now I wouldn't think of it. The geese would probably nip me for being on their lawn."

"I guess you do have a problem," Midge said.

"This spring the currants were getting ripe and we went away for two days," Mrs. Walcott continued. "When we got back they had stripped the bushes. I was furious. I was going to make jelly. They haven't eaten the blueberries or raspberries yet, but nothing would surprise me."

"I read someplace that farmers use geese to weed strawberries and tomatoes," I said. "They like the weeds but not the strawberries or tomatoes. But those were tame geese."

"I think their eating habits are about the same," Mrs. Walcott said. "I read that someplace too, but I think it is just a myth. Geese may not like strawberries, but after a flock of them have waddled through a strawberry patch, no one else would eat the strawberries either. We don't have any strawberries, anyway. However, I would like some solution to the general goose problem."

"Couldn't you just shoot off a shotgun and scare them?" Midge asked. "You wouldn't have to kill them."

"Possibly, but aside from the fact that John doesn't have a gun, I don't want to shoot around Mrs. Gerber's pond. She is a sweet, gentle soul, and much opposed to hunting. It *is* her pond, although I think she is beginning to get a little tired of the geese herself. I haven't wanted to upset her by going over to complain about them. What I would like is a quiet, effective way of eliminating them or at least cutting down on the number."

She glanced at her watch. "I have to be going. Give the matter some thought if your think tank has some spare time. I'd be happy to pay you for any workable suggestion."

She drove off and we went back to our desk. At least we had something else to think about. We postponed any more work on the health-food case and took up the question of geese.

"Do you suppose if we went over every day and threw rocks at them, they'd get the idea and leave?" Midge asked.

"Maybe," I said. "But geese are very stubborn. And they'd come back as soon as we quit throwing rocks. You couldn't go over there every day after school starts, and I certainly couldn't if I wasn't even in the United States. I doubt if Mrs. Walcott would want to go out every morning and throw rocks."

"Probably not," Midge admitted. "Besides, she doesn't look like she'd be very good at rock throwing. I'll just put rock throwing down as a poor possibility."

We talked over different ideas almost until lunchtime and came up with only one idea that was any good at all. We thought of getting a fox and keeping him near the pond. Geese are supposed to be sort of stupid, but they are smart enough to know they will be eaten if they stay near a fox. The trouble with that idea was that we didn't know where or how to capture a fox. There are some around our area but they are hard to see, let alone catch alive. Then we switched the idea around and substituted Agony for the fox.

"Agony chases a rabbit every time he sees one," Midge said. "Why couldn't he be trained to chase geese?"

"Maybe he could," I agreed. "But that would take quite a while. Why don't we break for lunch? I'll see what I can find out about natural enemies of geese before I come back."

Uncle Al has a number of books about wild animals and birds, and I looked through them after I had eaten, but I didn't find much that helped us. Big raccoons, if they get hungry enough in the winter, will kill chickens and even tackle a goose. The main enemy of geese seems to be man. The trouble is that when I read I get sidetracked and interested in something entirely different. I didn't make it back to the barn until three o'clock. Midge saw me and came over.

"I had a brilliant idea at lunch," she announced. "Pure genius. We had iced tea for lunch and Mom put mint in it. I don't like mint."

"I don't get the connection."

"We can put something in the pond that the geese don't like. They will get disgusted and fly away."

The idea was good but we couldn't think of what to use. If we used sprays that kill weeds they might kill the fish too. It had to be something nonpoisonous.

"How about tomato juice?" Midge asked. "If geese don't like tomatoes they probably don't like tomato juice."

"Probably not," I agreed. "But do you have any idea how much tomato juice we'd have to put in a pond before the geese would taste it? We'd have to buy most of the tomato juice in New Jersey."

"But she said it was a small pond," Midge objected.

"Even a small pond would take tons. We need something very powerful so we could dump in a tiny bottle and have it work."

"Let's ride over and take a look," she suggested.

That is what we did. Mrs. Walcott wasn't home, but we found the place without any trouble. And we found the geese. And as Mrs. Walcott had said, they weren't really wild at all. They moved away when we got near them, and when we got very close they simply walked into the pond, honking and hissing as they went. They *were* noisy!

I would hate to have a flock of them honking under my bedroom window at four-thirty in the morning. Also they were messy. Mrs. Gerber wouldn't need to fertilize the field around her pond for years.

All we had to do was look at the pond to know that tomato juice would never do. Agony had tagged along. He hadn't paid much attention to the geese but went sniffing around trying to find a rabbit. We called him over and pointed out the geese to him.

"Go get them, Agony," I said, pointing him toward the geese.

He didn't seem interested. Finally I picked up a stick and showed it to him. He is pretty good at going after a stick or ball. I threw it toward the geese.

"Fetch!" I ordered.

The stick landed right in the middle of the flock. It didn't seem to scare them much. They waddled away from it for a few feet and went right on feeding. Agony went after the stick. He was running full tilt, paying no attention to the geese. He picked up the stick and started back. As he turned one of the geese reached out and nipped him on the behind. He gave a surprised yip and came back even faster than he had gone. He put the stick down and then looked back at the geese.

"He thinks they are mean and so do I," Midge said.

We bicycled home feeling very discouraged. Either we needed a different idea or Agony needed a lot of training.

I explained the whole problem to Uncle Al at dinner. "Your first idea was the best," he said. "Shoot a few and have a nice goose dinner. The rest would be scared away.

And they would stay scared away if you made it an annual affair."

"I know Mrs. Gerber," Aunt Mabel said. "She'd be furious if anyone shot a goose on her place. I'm not certain she approves of swatting flies."

"Well, practice goose birth control," Uncle Al said. "When they make their nests, go around and break all the eggs. That should eventually discourage them."

"But we couldn't do that until next spring," I objected.

"I'm not certain it *would* discourage them," Aunt Mabel said. "Anyway, it would probably take three or four years before they got the idea they should build their nests someplace else."

"I guess training Agony to be a good goose chaser is the best idea," I said. "I wonder how long it would take. Who would know? Someone who trains hunting dogs?"

"I think it would take too long," Uncle Al said. "But I happen to know a man who used to train working retrievers. I am going over this evening to see him and deliver an insurance policy. You can ride along if you want and talk to him."

That seemed like a good idea, so about eight o'clock I put Agony in the car and we went to see this man, whose name was Allwood. He lives about six miles from Grover's Corner. When we drove in the yard four or five dogs began barking. It turned out they were Labrador retrievers which he kept in a kennel in back of the house. Mr. Allwood was a very pleasant man in his late sixties. When he and Uncle Al had finished their business about insurance, Uncle Al asked him about training dogs.

"My nephew here would like to discuss the possibility of training his beagle to chase geese."

"A beagle to chase geese?" he asked, as though I was out of my mind. "Why on earth would you want to do that? Beagles are born rabbit dogs. What you want for geese is a water dog. Besides, the dog is not supposed to chase geese; he's supposed to go get them and bring them back after you have shot them."

I explained why I wanted Agony to chase geese.

"That's simple," he said. "You don't want a dog to chase the geese. You want a swan."

"Are you serious?" Uncle Al asked.

"I certainly am," Mr. Allwood said. "I was in park maintenance and upkeep for forty years. We had dozens of ponds, and the geese were often a nuisance. A pair of adult swans are very jealous of their territory, especially during the nesting season. They are tough and nasty and they will drive Canada geese away. Now, on a lake, that simply means they chase the geese well away from their nesting site and what they consider their territory. But on a small pond, like a farm pond, they won't allow the geese to nest at all. They will chase everything away, including you if you scare easily."

"That sounds like exactly what we need," I said. "That's a great idea."

"How expensive are swans?" Uncle Al asked.

"Expensive," Mr. Allwood said. "An adult pair would be three or four hundred dollars. However, I happen to know a man at an arboretum in Philadelphia where they have more swans than they want. They have had great success raising young ones. You might get a bargain. But I want to warn you—they take a little care. You have to feed them now and then, especially in the winter, and during severe winter weather, you have to have some sort of shelter. Not much. Just a small shed open on one side, although it is best to have a way of locking them up. In very cold weather, when the pond freezes over, they have no way of escaping enemies like foxes or big dogs. When the water is not frozen they will spend most of their time on it and be safe."

I wrote down the name of the man in Philadelphia and thanked Mr. Allwood for the information.

"Be sure you don't get cygnets," he warned.

"What are cygnets?" I asked.

"The ugly duckling was a cygnet," he said. "It takes swans about three years to mature and start nesting. And until that time they won't do much of a job chasing the geese away."

"How noisy are swans?" Uncle Al asked.

"Not noisy at all," Mr. Allwood said. "The white swans you usually see swimming around on little ponds in public parks are called mute swans. They came originally from Europe. That's the kind of swan you will get from this place in Philadelphia."

I went out to the car and told Agony he had a reprieve. He didn't have to learn how to swim around chasing geese after all. He could keep on being just a plain old rabbit dog.

Thursday, August 29

The weather was great today. The sun was shining and there was a nice breeze. It was much too beautiful a day to stay inside, but I decided business had to come before pleasure. I wanted to know a lot more about swans before our think tank made any recommendations to Mrs. Walcott.

Uncle Al and Aunt Mabel read quite a bit, and they have more books than most people do. One whole wall of their living room is covered with books, many of them about wildlife, especially birds. I got out every book having anything to do with birds, the unabridged dictionary, and the one-volume encyclopedia. I went through them all very carefully, which didn't take long. There wasn't much about swans. About all I learned was that they are fairly close relatives to geese, only bigger.

About nine Aunt Mabel decided to go to Princeton to do some shopping, so I went along and went to the library. I did much better there. It seems North America has two native swans—the trumpeter swan and the whistling swan. The trumpeter swan is the biggest and toughest. It lives mostly in the western United States and Canada. It chases everything—geese, smaller swans, and even a lot of small animals away from its nest and later away from the cygnets or baby swans. All swans can make very loud noises, because of their long necks. I guess the long neck works like those long Alpine horns which you can hear for miles. The trumpeter swan was in danger of extinction a while back, but is now making a comeback. The whistling swan is a bit smaller than the trumpeter and its call is higher pitched and has a whistling sound to it. It can be pretty noisy. It nests in the Arctic and winters on both the Atlantic and Pacific coasts. You can see swans now and then in the bird refuge areas in New Jersey and Delaware. Both trumpeter and whistling swans are pure white.

Europe and Asia have a whooping swan, which is almost as big as the North American trumpeter swan. It is becoming quite scarce. Europe also has what is called the "mute swan," which, as Mr. Allwood said, is the one you usually see on ponds in parks. It isn't really mute at all. It can and does make some noise during nesting season if anything gets too close to its nest. However, it is much quieter than the other swans. Most of the time it doesn't make any noise at all, which is how it got its name. There is also a black swan in Australia and a white swan with a black neck in South America, but they are very rare here, so I didn't read much about them.

The mute swan was tamed in Europe centuries ago. The domesticated swans make even less noise than their wild cousins. During nesting season they may hiss a bit and once in a while give a honk, but most of the time they really are mute. They are the prettiest and most graceful of all swans. All the other swans have more or less straight necks, but mute swans have necks that make almost an S curve. Also they sort of puff out their wings, which makes them look very proud and impressive as they swim around. Although swans can walk very well, they spend most of their time swimming. They stay in the water much more than geese or ducks do. A few of the mute swans brought to this country from Europe have returned to the wild, but most of them prefer to stay in one place and have someone feed them. I didn't find out much about what they eat, but I did learn that they eat a lot of water grass and weeds. They swim around in the shallow water and reach down with that long neck to pull up a lot of food from the bottom.

It was about eleven when I got back from Princeton. I went down to the barn feeling like a real expert on the subject of swans. Midge was already there. She was scribbling on some scratch paper and had some sort of an account book in front of her.

"Hi," I said. "What are you doing?"

"Bringing our accounts up to date," she said. "After all, I am the treasurer. I have uncovered some surprising facts."

"Such as?"

"I think we should add a sideline to our think-tank business."

"What sort of sideline?"

"Changing tires," she said. "I was going over our expenses and most of the money we have in our treasury came from changing that tire yesterday. When you figure out the time we spent taking that poll and writing out our report, we made much more per hour changing the tire. And there was no expense at all."

"But changing tires is sort of accidental," I pointed out. "This was the first and only time I've known of anyone having a flat right here in Grover's Corner."

"We could scatter a few nails out in the road," she said.

I knew she didn't mean it. Midge likes action, and I could see she was getting a little discouraged about our think-tank business. We had had one success and one flop so far and yesterday hadn't looked very promising as far as getting Agony to chase geese was concerned.

"Well, I think Agony found the answer to our goose problem," I said. "At least he led me to the answer."

I told Midge about my trip to see Mr. Allwood and what he had suggested. She thought it was a terrific idea.

"Let's get on the bike and go see Mrs. Walcott," she said. "She'll love that idea!"

"There's just one trouble," I said. "Swans are very expensive. A pair might cost a couple of hundred dollars or even more."

"What do you suppose it would cost the Walcotts if he went out and bought a gun and some shells and shot a few geese? A pair of beautiful swans is a great investment! They can raise more swans and sell them to other people who have ponds. Maybe we can arrange to sell them for them and get a commission."

Mrs. Walcott was at home. We were invited into the house and given lemonade and cookies. I explained our solution to the goose problem and gave her the name and telephone number of the man in Philadelphia who had the swans for sale. She thought it was a wonderful idea.

"John has to go to Philadelphia tomorrow. I am going to call this afternoon and see if they still have the swans for sale. John could pick up the swans while he's there."

"From what I read they don't really get nasty to other birds like geese until nesting season," I warned. "It may be next spring before they chase all the geese away."

"The spring is the noisiest time, and if it takes that long for the swans to take over, we can survive," she said. "We are making no progress at all as it is. Anyhow, I will discuss all the details with this man whose name you gave me. I can't tell you how pleased I am with your suggestion. It's the perfect solution if it will work. Mrs. Gerber will be very touched if we give her a pair of beautiful swans. Now, how much do I owe your firm?"

Neither Midge nor I had thought about what our bill should be. I looked at Midge and she looked blank.

"Why don't we wait and see if this man still has swans and if he thinks they will do the job?" I suggested.

"If you want," she agreed. "But if this man doesn't have any swans I will find some someplace else. Let me give you some business advice. You have obviously spent some work and research on this matter, and if you come up with what you think is a good solution you should charge for it, and not wait until your customer decides whether or not he wants to use your solution."

We got on our bike and started home feeling pleased. Our score had improved quite a bit. Instead of one success and one failure we now had two hits and only one miss.

"You know, Mrs. Walcott is right," Midge said. "We should charge for our time when we think about a problem, whether or not our solution works. We should be like doctors and lawyers. A doctor charges you whether or not he cures you. You can die of whatever you have and he'd still send a bill. And if a lawyer defends you against some charge and you lose and go to jail, he still expects to be paid."

"That sounds all right, but how do you collect when something doesn't work? Suppose we sent the Shultz twins a bill for our services and for those spiders we bought. Do you think they would pay after all that trouble?"

"I suppose not," Midge admitted. "So from now on we get some money in advance. They call that a retainer fee."

It was lunchtime when we got home, but Deirdre was waiting for us. I knew I was getting a ham sandwich for lunch and the ham wasn't going to get any colder if it waited a while, so we stopped to find out what Deirdre wanted.

She didn't have to be reminded about her gum this time. She took out the huge wad of gum and parked it on the handlebars of her bike.

"I've been doing lots of work on kites and kite contests," she said.

I had forgotten that we had asked her to look up something about kites and kite-flying contests. In fact I had forgotten about Rodney's problem. I felt a little guilty, because he was our first client and we had done nothing at all on his case.

"Find out anything exciting?" Midge asked.

"Not much," Deirdre said. "There doesn't seem to be any standard set of rules the way there is for dog shows or athletic games. We can make our own rules. We can give a prize to the kite that is the prettiest, the one that is the most unusual, or the one that flies best. Or maybe we could give prizes for all three."

"That would be too expensive," I said. "Which would Rodney do the best?"

"Not in making the prettiest kite," Midge said promptly. "I was in art class with Rodney, and Rembrandt he ain't."

"Rodney's kites are great fliers," Deirdre said. "I think the prize should go to the kite that flies the best. He could win that."

"The thing that bothers me is, what does flying the best mean?" I asked. "Is that the kite that goes up the fastest, the one that stays up the longest, or the one that flies the highest?"

"I'd say the one that is the highest after so many minutes," Midge suggested.

We finally decided we would blow a whistle to start the contest. No kites could be launched before the whistle. Whichever kite was highest twenty minutes later would win. Then Deirdre brought up an even worse problem. How could you be sure which kite was really the highest? From one spot on the ground one would look the highest and from someplace else a different kite would seem higher. There were certain to be arguments.

"Maybe we should have a judge far away on a hill?" Midge suggested.

"A balloon would be better," I said. "There aren't any high hills near here."

"Maybe we could make a balloon," Midge said. "We made that balloon that took Agony and Siegfried the cat up. Remember?"

"I remember, but we'd need one twenty times that big."

"My dad knows a man who has a hot-air balloon," Deirdre said. "He sells rides in his balloon. He's just getting started, and maybe if he could advertise, or get a lot of publicity at our kite-flying contest, he would take up the judges."

"Terrific idea," Midge said, getting very excited. "I can see it all now—big crowds out in Mr. Baines's pasture, the air filled with kites, the balloon up above everyone, newspaper people snapping pictures, the band playing and the three of us in charge of it all."

When Midge gets enthusiastic about anything she is really enthusiastic. It was the same picture that she had described before, except now she had added a balloon and a band to the crowds and the kites. But if we could get a balloon maybe we might get some three-piece orchestra to come to our contest.

"That is a great idea, Deirdre," I said. "Find out if the

110

balloon man would be interested. Tell him he'll get lots of free publicity."

Lunch didn't take long because I got the ham sandwich that I expected. After lunch I helped Aunt Mabel in her garden for a while. She was taking out several clumps of iris and some other plants. Aunt Mabel is sort of plump to be much good at digging so I did the digging and the yanking while she did the directing and part of the puffing. It was after two-thirty when I got back to the barn. Midge was nowhere around.

We don't try to keep regular business hours at the barn but I like to be there a good part of the time each day in case some important customer should appear. Besides, the barn is a great place to hang out and a nice quiet spot to read. We have a little paper sign that Midge made that says OUT ON CONSULTATION—BE BACK SHORTLY and gives our telephone number. We tape the sign inside the window near the door. I took the sign down when I arrived and went over to the desk to work on our kite-flying contest.

I had brought a pad of sketching paper, so I sketched a poster announcing the contest. Across the top of the page, in a sort of arc, I put GREAT KITE-FLYING CONTEST in big letters. Beneath it I sketched seven or eight kids flying kites. I like lettering and that looked fairly good, but I am not much at drawing people. The kids flying kites looked more like vultures about to swoop down on something. I started over with a fresh piece of paper and it was still poor. Finally I gave up on the sketch. I worked on the rest of the poster for about an hour. When I finished it looked like this:

GREAT KITE-FLYING CONTEST

GROVER'S CORNER EXTRAORDINARY KITE COMPETITION

—GRAND PRIZE $50—

Saturday, September 14, 3:00 P.M.
(In case of rain or complete lack of wind the contest
will be postponed to Sunday, September 15, same time)

CONTEST TO BE HELD IN MR. BAINES'S COW PASTURE—
GROVER'S CORNER, N.J.

*All entrants must design, make, and fly their own kites.
See Margaret Glass for rules and entry blanks. 446-0888*

Of course, this was only a first draft. I hadn't talked to
Midge about it at all, and we didn't know yet if Mr. Baines
would let us have the contest in his cow pasture. The fifty-
dollar grand prize I had put in just for effect. We didn't
have anything like fifty dollars in the treasury, but we
needed to offer a prize of some kind to make the contest
interesting. Except for the sketch, the poster looked good
when I finished. I put it aside and began working on the
rules. I could think of only eight.

1. Entrants must be no older than sixteen.
2. All entrants must design and build their own kites.
   Any help from adults will disqualify them.
3. No kite can have a dimension greater than sixty
   inches.
4. Kites may be with or without tails.

112

5. Kites must be constructed of wood, string, paper, and glue. Thin-film plastic may be substituted for paper if desired.
6. Each contestant must fly his own kite.
7. A contestant may bring an assistant to hold his kite during launching. For those who do not have an assistant, the contest officials will provide one.
8. The judges' decision will be final. There will be only one prize.

It was almost five o'clock when I finished. I was looking over the rules when Midge appeared.

"Been shopping with my mom," she said. "Any new business?"

"None. I've been working on a poster for our kite-flying contest. What do you think of this?"

She took my rough draft and looked at it thoughtfully. "Hmmm," she said. "What are all these funny-looking marks? They look like spiders and spider webs."

"That's supposed to be kids flying kites," I said. "We need an artist who can draw people."

"Mom can draw a little. I'll ask her. Otherwise I think it's great! And that grand prize of fifty dollars is terrific! That ought to drag in lots of kites."

"There's one little problem," I said. "We don't have fifty dollars."

Midge waved her hand. "That's easy. We just charge an entry fee of five dollars. If we have more than ten kites entered we make money. And I'll bet with that prize we'll have a lot more than ten."

We talked about the date for a while, but September 14 is about the only date possible. People need at least ten days or so to design and make their kites, and we need that much time to get posters out, get articles in the newspaper, and make all the arrangements. School will have started before the contest so Saturday and Sunday are the only practical days. And if we wait much later than the fourteenth I will be on my way to the Philippines.

"I'll see Mr. Baines tomorrow," Midge promised. "And I'll call Deirdre tonight and tell her to be here for a big conference in the morning."

Friday, August 30

We are making real progress with our kite-flying contest. Midge went to see Mr. Baines this morning, and he said we could use his big pasture. The pasture runs in back of the barn as well as all the houses on that side of the road. The gate to the pasture is on the other side of Uncle Al's house. The shoulder is fairly wide there, so people will be able to park beside the road.

Midge had just come back from seeing Mr. Baines when Deirdre telephoned. She was very excited about something, but we couldn't learn why because she forgot to take the gum out of her mouth. Midge did manage to make out that she was on the way over on her bike. She must have pedaled like mad, because in less than ten minutes she came bursting into the barn. Midge ripped a clean sheet of paper from her note pad and put it on the table.

"You can park your gum there," she said.

"Guess what?" Deirdre said after she had parked her gum. "Mr. Matuska is going to bring his balloon and he will take up the judge during the contest!"

"Wow!" Midge said. "Now we have to have a band."

"There's just one thing," Deirdre said. "He said to be sure and check with whoever owns the field where you have the contest."

"That's Mr. Baines," Midge said. "I saw him this morning and everything is all set."

"Did you tell him you were going to have a big hot-air balloon?"

"No. But what's the difference—kites or balloons?"

"Lots of farmers don't like balloons," Deirdre said.

"Why?" I asked.

"Mr. Matuska said quite a few balloons have come down in the middle of fields where there are crops like corn, soy beans, or oats. When they let the air out of their balloon at the end of a flight and it covers a big area, it mashes any growing crops flat. And dairy farmers claim that low-flying balloons scare their cows."

"You mean cows look up in the sky and get scared of a balloon?" Midge asked. "That seems sort of silly to me. Most cows I've seen are always looking down at the grass they're eating."

"They hear the balloon and look up," Deirdre said. "Hot-air balloons are noisy. Do you know what keeps the air hot in a big balloon?"

116

"Unless it's the passengers talking, I give up," Midge said.

"Propane," I said. Last summer a balloon came floating over Grover's Corner, and Uncle Al and I went out to watch it. He explained how they work.

"Hot air is lighter than cold air and so the balloon stays up because the air inside the bag is warmer and lighter than the air outside," I said. "But they have to keep it warm. They have a propane tank and a torch that shoots a flame right up into the big hole in the bottom of the balloon."

"Yep," Deirdre agreed. "The flame is on a minute or so and then off a minute. You can hear it roar half a mile away. Our dog always gets scared and hides under the sofa. Balloons around here usually go up in the late afternoon, which is fine for our kite-flying contest. The wind is best around four or so—not too strong but enough to move the balloon along. When a balloon is drifting low over a pasture, naturally the cows get scared. Sometimes they run into fences. And they are still upset when they are milked an hour or so later."

"We better go talk to Mr. Baines," Midge said. "Since Mr. Matuska wants to go up from the pasture and not come down in it, we should be all right. And he won't have any cows in that pasture then. Still, we'd better go and make sure."

We all decided to go. We walked down the road to Mr. Baines's house. His house is well back from the road and down a long lane. Halfway there, Deirdre remembered that she had left her gum in our office. She wanted to go back to get it.

"Do your jaw muscles good to have a rest," Midge said.

"Suppose someone comes and steals it?" she objected.

"Our insurance will probably cover it," I said with a straight face. "Stolen gum would be replaced, wouldn't it, Midge?"

"Sure," Midge said. "With an equal-sized wad of used gum."

It was a good thing we convinced her to go on with us instead of back for her gum, because a minute later she had a great idea. Deirdre is smart.

"Look, if you think Mr. Baines might object to a balloon in his pasture, maybe it would be smart to ask him to be the judge before we bring up the matter of the balloon."

"Perfect," Midge agreed. "That will make him feel good, and besides, he would make a great judge. He looks dignified and honest."

Mr. Baines didn't look very dignified when we found him. He was giving worm medicine to his sheep. He had a little plastic device which held a huge pill of worm medicine at one end. He would catch a sheep, shove the pill way back in its throat, and then press a trigger which released the pill. The sheep didn't like it at all and were struggling and refusing to open their mouths. We waited until he was finished, which was only a few minutes.

"Well, what can I do for you young folks?" he asked.

I guess Mr. Baines is in his sixties. He has white hair where he has hair, bright blue eyes, and a big stomach like my Uncle Al. As Uncle Al would say, he's not fat—just portly. His face is big and round and he smiles a lot.

118

Midge has known Mr. Baines all her life, so we had elected her to do the talking.

"We've come to ask a big favor of you, Mr. Baines," she said. "We need a judge for our great kite-flying contest on September 14. We want someone who doesn't have any relatives in the contest and who is known to be fair. So we thought of you."

Mr. Baines was very pleased. His face broke into a big smile. "It's real nice of you to ask me, Margaret, but I don't know a thing about kites."

"We don't know much either," I said. "There don't seem to be any standard rules for kite-flying contests, so we made up our own. The kite that is the highest after twenty minutes wins."

"And there is no arguing with the judge's decision," Midge said.

"It might be sort of difficult from the ground to tell which one is the highest," Mr. Baines said.

"We've thought of that," Midge said proudly. "We have arranged to have a hot-air balloon. The judge will be in the balloon and will be able to see perfectly. Of course, the balloon will be tethered, so it can't drift away."

"Balloon," Mr. Baines said, his eyes twinkling. "Now that sounds mighty interesting. Everytime I see one of those drifting over, I think maybe I'd like to take a ride sometime."

"Then you'll be our judge? That's great!" Midge said, very pleased. If Mr. Baines was willing to go up in a balloon he certainly wouldn't object to having one in his pasture.

"Well, I might on one condition," he said cautiously.

"What's that?" I asked.

"That not a word about my going up in a balloon is to be mentioned to my wife. She is of the opinion that a person ought to keep one foot on the ground. Had a terrible time getting her to fly out to Chicago for our daughter's wedding. If there had been time, I think she would have preferred walking."

We promised to say nothing to Mrs. Baines and went home. Deirdre's gum was still on the paper when we got back to the barn. We worked until noon jotting down things to tell the newspaper about our great kite-flying contest. Midge is going to Princeton in the morning with her mother. We agreed to tell the paper that we were going to have a balloon to help judge the contest but not to say that the judge was actually going up in the balloon. We knew that Mrs. Baines would read the paper. Midge wanted to add that we were going to have a band, but since we didn't know where we could get a band, much less pay for it, we settled for saying there would be music. We hope we can borrow a couple of speakers, a powerful amplifier, and a tape deck somewhere.

Deirdre left to go home at twelve-thirty, and Midge and I were about to do the same when a little sports car zipped in off the road and a woman hopped out. I do mean hopped, because she moved like a little bird. She cocked her head to one side and looked up at our sign. Then she started toward the door.

"Hello," she said, when she reached the open door. "Are you two Reed and Glass?"

"The very ones," I said.

"Hmmm," she said doubtfully. "You are a little younger than I had expected."

She was much older than I had expected for someone who was driving a flashy little sports car and moving around the way she did. Her hair was cut quite short and was sort of salt and pepper. Her face was very tanned and full of wrinkles.

"Jenny Walcott tells me that you two are very bright and capable," she said, as though not expecting any reply from us about how young we were. "And I guess that is what is important, not your age. I need some help for a few days."

"What sort of help?" I asked.

"Well, suddenly and unexpectedly I have had a granddaughter dumped in my lap. My daughter and her husband had to make an emergency trip to Ohio and left their daughter with me. It isn't that I don't enjoy her visiting me, but this was unexpected. Tomorrow I have to attend a fund-raising committee meeting in Princeton, the next day I will be gone all day judging a dog show, and the following day I arranged to go to a special lecture at the Metropolitan Museum in New York."

"You would like someone to baby-sit for three days, I take it?" I asked.

"Henry and I ran a baby-sitting service for a while," Midge said. "We are experienced."

"You couldn't exactly call it baby-sitting," she said. "Entertaining would be more accurate."

"How old is this granddaughter?" Midge asked suspiciously.

"Sixteen."

"Sixteen! Why that's a lot older even than Henry," Midge said.

"I daresay. That's why I was a little taken aback when I saw how young you two are."

"Is there something wrong with your granddaughter?" I asked. I tried to make my voice sound sympathetic. After all, there must be something wrong with a sixteen-year-old who needs a baby-sitter.

The woman gave a short laugh. "Not in the way you mean. In fact she is a very bright and a very attractive girl. It's just that she's impossible. She's at that age and stage when she can only be described as a pain in the neck. I guess almost all teenage girls are at one point or another."

"I've heard that about them," I said and moved back to be safe in case Midge kicked me.

"What does she do that's so awful?" Midge asked.

"Well, she is in a languid, bored phase at the moment," she said. "By the way, I am Agatha Martin. I live on the same road as the Walcotts—a small stone house near the road."

"I think I know it," Midge said. "Climbing vines all over one end."

"That's right," Mrs. Martin said. "But to get back to my problem—while I dearly love my granddaughter, the few times I have been with her for the past six months, I could think of little to do with her except give her a healthy kick. I am hopelessly out of date as far as she is concerned—sweet but senile. And the entire Princeton area is a hick town full of yokels in her estimation."

"Where is she from?" I asked.

"Westport, Connecticut. While Westport is a very nice suburb, it is certainly no more sophisticated than Princeton and probably doesn't offer half the cultural advantages. Anyhow, my son and his wife were taking Heloise to look at several colleges around here, since she will be going to college in another year. When this emergency in Ohio arose, they left her with me. The trouble is that I am very busy with my own affairs, all of which are absorbing to me but hopelessly fuddy-duddy to Heloise. Otherwise I would take her along. The simple fact of the matter is that I am not in her age group—I am her grandmother. And I have neither the time nor inclination to take up such things as rock-and-roll and wind scooting."

"Do you mean wind surfing?" I asked. "That's great!"

"No doubt it is. I loved downhill skiing when I was sixteen. Anyhow, here I am with all sorts of important engagements and the sudden job of entertaining her. I haven't the slightest idea of what a young lady her age might be interested in. So I am looking for help."

"Just what sort of help do you want?" I asked. "Advice about things she might like to do, or do you want us to take over the job of entertaining her?"

"Nothing would suit me better than for you to take over the entire responsibility," Mrs. Martin said. "Everything I suggest is either 'boring' or 'passé.' And that is apparently what I am."

"We could probably think up some things she'd enjoy doing, but most of them would be in Princeton or New Hope or places like that. We'd need transportation,"

Midge pointed out. "Neither Henry nor I has a driver's license."

"I suspected that," Mrs. Martin said. "Neither has Heloise. I could help out now and then. I could drive you to various places when my schedule permits. As far as Princeton or Lawrenceville are concerned, both have taxis."

"They're expensive," Midge said.

"I know, but less expensive than scrapping my entire schedule. If I gave you money so that you could buy Cokes and ice cream and pizzas, go to the movies, go out to dinner one night, and take taxis when necessary, do you think you could dream up things to keep her occupied for the next three days?"

"Do you mean morning, afternoon, and evening?" I asked. It seemed like a big order to me. I didn't think much of being a baby-sitter for a sixteen-year-old girl. In fact I don't think much of most sixteen-year-old girls.

"Well, as I mentioned, Heloise is playing the role of the sophisticated Lady of the Manor at the moment. So she sleeps late, thank goodness. Don't worry about the mornings. So that means tomorrow afternoon. Tomorrow evening we are invited out to dinner. Sunday, I would be grateful if you could entertain her both afternoon and evening—I won't be back before nine or ten. On Monday, which is Labor Day, I would like you to think up something for the afternoon. I will pick her up about dinner time wherever you say."

"This is rather sudden, but we will get right to work on it and think up something," Midge said confidently.

I wasn't so certain. Sixteen-year-old girls can be very

superior about things. I was about to say we would talk matters over before definitely taking the job, but Mrs. Martin opened her purse and took out two twenty-dollar bills.

"Keep a rough account of what you spend and when you get low I will give you some more."

"I'll keep track and Henry can pay the bills," Midge said. "It looks better if the man pays the bills, especially if she is putting on a Lady of the Manor act."

"That's a good point," Mrs. Martin agreed.

"Besides, Henry is a sophisticated traveler. He's been to all sorts of cities," Midge said, with a wave of her hand. She had a little trouble pronouncing sophisticated, but I don't think Mrs. Martin noticed.

"Yes?" Mrs. Martin said. "What cities?"

"London, Paris, Rome, Athens, Tokyo, Hong Kong, and Singapore."

"He has been around," Mrs. Martin said. "How did you happen to travel so much, Henry?"

"My father is in the diplomatic service," I said.

"I see," she said. She got up to leave.

I didn't feel too happy. There I sat with forty whole dollars in my hand. It was either give it back or go ahead with this crazy scheme. I could see that Midge was all for going ahead.

"We'll think of some things to do this afternoon and then we'll call you," I said.

"That would be fine." She pulled out a little pad and wrote her name and telephone number and 6:30. "Call me about six-thirty and you'll reach me. Now tomorrow

I can probably drive you any place within ten miles or so between twelve-thirty and one-thirty. You will have to work out the return transportation—a taxi or something."

She went to the door. "Remember, I am not asking you to like Heloise—just to keep her reasonably entertained and out of my hair."

She hurried out, got in her little car, and went zooming up the road. I sat where I was, holding the money.

"I think we have got ourselves in a real mess," I said. "Trying to entertain a stuck-up sixteen-year-old girl is not only crazy, it is stupid and dangerous."

"Henry Reed, you are a scaredy cat!" Midge said. "You are afraid of trying something different."

"I'm scared of a sixteen-year-old who thinks everything is passé," I said. "She's *too* different. And when a grandmother says her own granddaughter is impossible, look out!"

"What does 'passé' mean?" Midge asked.

"Out of date, behind the times."

"Is that all?" Midge sniffed. "Just remember, Henry, that you and I are later models than she is by several years. So we are more up to date than she is. Heloise! That's a silly name. I hope I don't giggle when I say it. Boy, oh boy, oh boy! What a setup! Ever since the first time I saw my dad use his credit card I have wanted one of my own. Only this is much better than a credit card. We can just go ahead and spend and no bills will come in."

"Let's start thinking of things to do," I suggested. Midge gets off the subject at times, and you have to drag her back.

"All right. Tomorrow let's fly to Acapulco," she said. "I've always wanted to go to Acapulco. Now I can finally afford it."

"Be serious," I said.

"All right, let's go talk to my mom. She has great ideas and she knows what's going on around here."

I went home for lunch first and then went to Midge's house. Mrs. Glass was busy repotting some house plants. Midge had already told her about our new job.

"It's too bad we didn't know about this sooner, as we have already made some plans for part of the weekend," Mrs. Glass said. "Most people have, you know—it's Labor Day weekend. But I suppose you could cancel your tubing expedition, Margaret, and go to the seashore. She might like that."

"No. Never, never, never, never," Midge said firmly. "Tubing is a tradition! I always do that before I go back to school. I've done that almost forever."

"Well, three years," Mrs. Glass said with a smile.

"What is tubing?" I asked.

"You put on your bathing suit, and then you get in a great big inner tube and you float down the Delaware River," Mrs. Glass explained. "You bump your behind on rocks, you get all scratched, you are sunburned, you get upset in the rapids and all bruised. For some strange reason Midge loves it."

"It's great. Unbelievable! Wonderful!" Midge said. "We take a picnic lunch along and eat it somewhere—maybe on an island. You've never been on a tubing expedition, Henry. You'll love it. Monday is all decided. Heloise will just have to go with us."

"She might find it childish as well as rough," Mrs. Glass said doubtfully.

"She will just have to like it," Midge said. "We will think up something real refined and ladylike for tomorrow and Sunday. Monday she roughs it."

"All right, that takes care of Monday," Mrs. Glass said. "Let's go back to tomorrow and Sunday. You might take her swimming at that pool off Witherspoon. It's a very nice pool, and there are always lots of young people your age there. Also, there is a fine exhibit at the University Art Museum, and I think a new show at Squibbs."

"I think a museum would be better than swimming, don't you, Henry?" Midge asked.

"I'd rather go swimming," I said.

"So would I," Midge said. "But business before pleasure. If this Heloise is so lah-de-dah she'll go for anything she thinks is cultured and refined. Besides, on Monday she is going to get enough water to last her for quite a while."

"Look in the paper," Mrs. Glass said. "There's a whole section on what to do in this area."

We spent about ten minutes looking through the section on the theater, dance, museums, art shows, sports events, and places to eat. While Midge was reading about some craft show, I looked through the places to eat.

"That looks good for Sunday night," I said, pointing to an ad.

Midge read the advertisement aloud. "Enjoy a delicious dinner and excellent theater at one and the same time at the Old Mill Pond Inn. Eat succulent lobster or delicious

128

roast beef while you thrill to the 'Trials and Tribulations of Tessie,' an old-fashioned melodrama presented by the talented Tri-State Players. Hiss, applaud, boo, or cheer as the mood strikes you. The show begins promptly at seven-fifteen. Reservations suggested."

"That sounds great!" Midge said.

"Do you think it would be very expensive?" I asked.

"You forget, we have an unlimited expense account," Midge said with a wave of her hand.

"Henry is right," Mrs. Glass said. "You really shouldn't commit yourselves to anything outrageously expensive. I don't imagine it will be that. Why don't you call and find out and also see if you can get reservations? If you can, it would probably work out very well and we could take you there and bring you back."

I didn't much want to call. I'd never made reservations at a restaurant before, but I wasn't going to tell Midge that. The woman who answered had a very nice voice. She said that the cost depended on what you ate but that most of the entrees were between fifteen and twenty dollars. We should be there at seven and the show would be over about nine forty-five. I put my hand over the telephone and explained to Midge and her mother. They were both in favor, so I made reservations.

"That's reasonable enough for a restaurant like that, especially since it includes a show," Mrs. Glass said. "Now, here's the plan. I accepted an invitation to go over to the Edelsons' Sunday afternoon and stay for dinner. We could drop you in New Hope on our way, about mid-afternoon, I would say. You could spend the afternoon looking around

New Hope. Do you know anything about New Hope, Henry?"

"Just where it is. I drove through it once with Uncle Al."

"Well, it's quite a tourist attraction. It's filled with unusual shops, there is a summer theater there, and at this time of year on a weekend it is jammed with tourists. I think one of the main attractions is that they all look at each other. I'm sure this Heloise would enjoy poking through all those unusual little shops."

I was sure I wouldn't. I hate shopping. My feet always get tired. But as Midge had just said, business comes before pleasure. Besides, I didn't have any better ideas.

"There is a taxi in New Hope. You should make reservations ahead of time for it to take you to the restaurant. It's only a couple of miles from New Hope. And we will pick you up when the show is over."

"This gets more exciting all the time," Midge said enthusiastically. "Going out to dinner in a taxi and seeing a show. Don't you think I ought to have a new dress for dinner and the theater?"

"If you pay for it," Mrs. Glass said. "And don't plan on taking it out of your so-called expense account."

Midge shrugged. "Well, it was a thought. Now that leaves only tomorrow—Saturday. And we have sort of settled on a museum."

"I know," Mrs. Glass said. "The Hopewell Museum. There is an arts and crafts show outside on the lawn. If it rains it will be inside. You can see that and also the museum."

130

"I don't think I've ever been to the Hopewell Museum," Midge said.

"You make me feel guilty," Mrs. Glass said. "It's a delightful place, and very unusual for a town the size of Hopewell. It is a museum of early life in America—furniture, dishes, guns, glassware, dolls, and a very fine collection of costumes. There is even a natural history room with a big stuffed eagle that was shot long ago near Hopewell. Also, there is a big room of Indian items that you'll like, Henry."

"Sounds good," Midge said. "What about transportation?"

"This Mrs. Martin can take you there, I think you mentioned," Mrs. Glass said. "Maybe Mrs. Rollins can bring you back."

"Mrs. Rollins? Why her?"

"Because she does volunteer work there, mending some of their early dresses. And also she will be keeping an eye on the area where she is working. In the past few months some things have disappeared."

"What sort of things?" I asked. "I hope not the stuffed eagle."

"No. Things somewhat smaller and easier to carry. Pictures, paintings, and several samplers."

Neither Midge nor I knew what a sampler was.

"Well, in Colonial days, all young girls were taught to embroider. They often embroidered the alphabet on a piece of fine linen, or something such as 'God Bless Our Home.' If they did it nicely, their parents framed the work and hung it on the wall. The Hopewell Museum has a number of delightful samplers done by little girls who lived long ago. Girls much younger than you, Margaret."

"Hmmm," Midge said. "What do you think, Henry?"

"Sounds all right," I said. I am not very keen about china and glass, but the Indian exhibits sounded interesting.

"The craft show starts at two," Mrs. Glass said. "There is a nice place not far away to have lunch. You could eat a leisurely lunch and then spend the rest of the afternoon at the museum."

I waited until six-thirty and then I called Mrs. Martin. I had written it all down so I was able to give her the schedule in a very businesslike way—Saturday, Sunday, and Monday. When I got to Monday I didn't give her too many details. I just said an all-day outing on the Delaware, and didn't mention that her highbrow granddaughter was going to go bumping and splashing over the rocks.

"Sounds like an absolutely marvelous plan," Mrs. Martin said enthusiastically. "I can't tell you how grateful I am. If you will do a little figuring, Henry, and let me know tomorrow about how much you think you will spend, I will give you enough to cover it all. The dinner on Sunday night alone, which sounds wonderful, will take more than I've given you."

I said I would do that, and she promised to pick us up the next day about one and take us to Hopewell. I hope this Heloise appreciates all the thinking we have put in on this job. I'm not looking forward to tagging along with two girls while they wander through the shops in New Hope. Midge is the smartest girl I know but even she likes to go shopping. My father says women have different kind of feet than men. He claims men's feet were designed centuries ago to chase down animals for food while women's feet were designed to chase bargains.

Saturday, August 31

Well, we got through the first day of entertaining Heloise.
It wasn't nearly as bad as I expected. The outdoor craft
show was interesting, the Hopewell Museum was great,
our lunch was good, and Heloise was just as impossible
as her grandmother warned.

Mrs. Martin picked us up a little before one o'clock.
We all crowded into that little car of hers and she dropped
us off in Hopewell a few minutes after one. I don't think
Heloise was a bit pleased to see Midge and me. My guess
is that Mrs. Martin hadn't told her that we were several
years younger than she was. She looked at us as though
we were some variety of worm, and when Mrs. Martin
introduced us she said "hello" as though that one word
tired her out completely.

Heloise is a pretty girl. She has long brown hair, blue eyes, and a nice smile when she finds the energy to smile. That isn't often, because most of the time she is too busy being bored. She is an inch or two taller than me and at least four inches taller than Midge, which may be the reason she keeps acting as though we are little kids. Probably the best way to describe her is to say that she is a sixteen-year-old pretending she is twenty. She wears eye shadow, a lot of lipstick, eyebrow pencil, and some awful smelly perfume.

Mrs. Glass told us where to eat lunch. It was a little place that serves only lunch and the food was very good. Heloise pretended there was nothing on the menu that she wanted, but she certainly didn't eat that way when the food arrived. I think she was annoyed to have me pay the bill. I think I did it very well. I acted as though I had paid lots and lots of restaurant checks. Mrs. Glass had said that we should leave a tip and I figured out the amount in my head. Midge offered me a pencil but I didn't need it.

The craft show was in full swing by the time we got to the museum. The Hopewell Museum has a big lawn and there were exhibits in front, on both sides, and in back. One woman was spinning yarn from sheep's wool, another was weaving a shawl, a man demonstrated how to put cane seats in chairs, and a woman was using a potter's wheel to make bowls and plates. There was a very interesting demonstration of early cooking over an open fire where the woman made cornmeal muffins using old iron implements. There was an art show on the right side of the museum, and in the back a woman was making candles using molds from the museum and a blacksmith had set up a forge and was making horseshoes.

"Very interesting and quaint," Heloise said in a weary voice. "Sort of boring because I've seen it all a number of times before. There's a craft show in Greenwich each year like this, only much larger, of course."

"Of course," Midge said in a voice that was even more bored.

The blacksmith heated a piece of iron red hot and began hammering it into a fancy hinge. I stood watching, but Heloise and Midge moved on to where the woman was making candles. After a while Midge came over and poked me in the ribs with her elbow. Heloise was still at the candle exhibit.

"She's a fake," Midge whispered. "She's interested in how to make those candles, but she won't let on that she doesn't know all about it. So instead of asking questions herself she keeps telling me to ask them. I wouldn't mind, except that when I do, she pretends she isn't interested and is just waiting around to let me ask silly questions."

The museum opened at three and we went inside. Most of the people were still outside and we had the place pretty much to ourselves. The second room on the left had some china and glass and a lot of books. I started to look at the titles.

"Some of them are reference books about items that we have," a woman told us. "But most of them are genealogies."

"What are genealogies?" Midge asked.

"Books about family history," Heloise said with a pitying smile at how dumb Midge was. "If you come from a family that has a genealogy, you can look up who your ancestors were."

"We have genealogies on the Harts, the Goldens, the Stouts—"

"My grandmother on my father's side was a Stout," Heloise interrupted. "How could I find out if she came from the Hopewell Stouts?"

The woman was delighted to have someone interested, and she and Heloise were soon deep in a book. I don't know if Heloise was really interested or just thought looking up her ancestors was cultured and adult. We stayed around for several minutes, but we could see that she was going to be a while. We told her we would be wandering through the rest of the museum and went on.

We went upstairs and looked at a music room that had an old piano, an organ, and a wonderful old music box. Beyond that was the second floor of the museum addition, where there was a display of costumes.

"Hi, Mrs. Rollins," Midge said as we stepped through the door.

"Hello, Margaret," Mrs. Rollins said. "Enjoying yourself?"

"Well, I'm enjoying the museum," Midge said. "What are you doing?"

Mrs. Rollins was on her knees beside a mannequin, which was wearing a cream-colored dress that came down to the floor. Mrs. Rollins was trying to do something with the hem and the back and was having quite a bit of trouble. Her main problem was that she was much too fat to be crawling around on her knees as she worked on the dress.

"They have some lovely old dresses here," she said, puffing a little. "I took this home and cleaned it by hand and now I'm trying to put the hem in and fix a tuck in the back so it will fit properly on the mannequin. Is this your friend Henry, Margaret?"

I was introduced to Mrs. Rollins. She said hello and then went back to the dress.

"I think it is a little too high in back now," Midge said, bending down near the floor to look.

"Now if I could just bend over like that I wouldn't have to crawl around on my knees," Mrs. Rollins said. She looked up at Midge and her eyebrows went up. "You know, you are just about the exact size, Margaret. How would you like to slip this dress on and stand up on that chair? I could fix it in no time then."

"All right," Midge said agreeably. "How old is that dress?"

"Almost two hundred years. It was a wedding dress. And the bride who wore it made that sampler over there."

She nodded toward the framed embroidery hanging on the wall a few feet away.

"Fun," Midge said. She was wearing shorts and a blouse, so she just slipped the dress on over her clothes. Mrs. Rollins was right, the dress fit Midge perfectly. She climbed up on the chair that Mrs. Rollins had been using and turned around slowly while Mrs. Rollins pinned the hem of the dress.

"That looks good," she said. "Just stand over there and let me look at it from a bit further away."

Midge got down from the chair and went over to stand beside the male mannequin. I guess he was supposed to be the groom. Just then there was a call from the bottom of the stairs.

"Ella, telephone!"

"Coming," Mrs. Rollins said. "I'll be back in a few minutes. If that dress gets too hot, Margaret, take it off. I would appreciate it if you would sort of keep an eye on this room. A few things have been missing lately."

"Mom mentioned that," Midge said. "I'll stay here until you get back."

Mrs. Rollins went huffing and puffing down the stairs. From her speed I had my doubts that she would be back in a few minutes.

"Do I look like a Colonial bride?" Midge asked, posing beside the male mannequin.

The long dress did make her look a lot older than she usually does, but she still looked too young to be a bride. Her hair was long enough, but it was in a ponytail.

"I don't think you would fool anyone," I said. "They didn't wear their hair the way you do."

The dummy that had been wearing the dress had been set to one side by Mrs. Rollins. It had a wig of long, dark brown hair. Midge went over and removed the wig and put it on her own head. It changed her looks completely. I would never have recognized her.

"Pretty good," I said. "You could pass for a dummy any time."

"I'll bet that if I stood perfectly still, anyone passing through wouldn't know I was alive," she said.

"I think someone is coming," I said. "I'll go up there just outside the music room where I can watch. You stand perfectly still and we'll see if they notice. I hope it's Heloise."

"So do I," Midge said. "Maybe when she's looking the other way I can kick her and then freeze in my pose. She won't know what happened."

I hurried up the two or three steps and ducked around the edge of the doorway. Whoever was coming up the back stairs reached the top and then stopped to look back at the quilt hanging on the wall by the stairs. Finally I peeked around. It wasn't Heloise but a small slender woman wearing a gray suit and carrying a big purse. Midge made a face at me but stood perfectly still.

The visitor wandered over to look at the first room. She was taking her time, and I had my doubts that Midge could stand still much longer. Finally she finished looking at the first two rooms and moved to the third, which was directly opposite Midge. She was standing with her back toward Midge when a fly landed on Midge's nose. I didn't think she could possibly stand that for long, but after wrinkling her nose several times she managed to blow some air up by her nose and scared it away. Just then the woman began to turn, and if she turned far enough she was sure to see me, so I ducked out of sight.

I waited for several minutes and heard nothing. I had just decided to stroll down into the room as though I was just another visitor and see what was going on when I heard Midge say in a hollow, ghostly voice, "Don't steal my sampler. I'll haunt you."

140

I looked through the door just in time to see the back of the woman. She was running for the stairs. She went clattering down them and bumped into someone. There was a grunt followed by a loud "Ouch."

"Stop her!" Midge shouted. "She tried to take the sampler!" We both rushed to look over the banister. The woman in the gray suit was sprawled at the bottom of the stairs, looking dazed and confused. Standing almost over her, and looking confused but not at all dazed, was Mrs. Rollins. The woman had bumped into Mrs. Rollins on her dash down the stairs, and when you hit Mrs. Rollins, you *know* that you have hit something.

"What is going on?" Mrs. Rollins asked.

"I was standing where you left me, pretending to be a model, and that woman took the sampler off the wall. She started to put it in that big purse of hers and I told her not to steal it. She dropped it and ran away."

The woman still seemed confused. Midge had taken off the wig and from below the woman couldn't see much except a girl with a ponytail and lots of freckles looking down.

"There is a policeman outside," Mrs. Rollins said firmly. "Let's go talk this over with him. Margaret, will you please come with me? Henry, would you stay there and keep an eye on things? It seems we need it."

I would much rather have gone outside to see what happened, but there was nothing to do but stay and guard things. I walked back and forth for at least ten minutes. Only two people came through—a middle-aged woman who said, "My, My," at everything she saw, and a man—

probably her husband—who wasn't interested at all. I think he would have much rather been home watching a ball game. Finally Midge came back.

"What happened?" I asked.

"Not much," Midge said. "I guess I'm a heroine of some kind but I don't feel very good about it."

"Why?"

"The woman started crying while we were talking to the policeman," Midge said. "She was really upset. She confessed to taking a lot more things. Finally he took her away. I guess he took her home."

"Did you see Heloise?" I asked. "What did she think of all the excitement? Bored with it all?"

"She was still sitting in that room reading about her ancestors," Midge said.

Mrs. Rollins came back a few minutes later. She didn't have much to add to what Midge had told me, so we went on looking through the museum. We were on the top floor when Heloise finally caught up with us. She insisted on telling us all about dozens of ancestors of hers and really didn't look at most of the exhibits. There was a great exhibit of dozens and dozens of beetles in the natural-history room all arranged according to size. I'd never seen a collection like it, but when I pointed it out to Heloise, she just said "Ugh, dead bugs!" and went right on talking about ancestors. I felt like telling her that all the ancestors she was talking about were dead too, but I didn't. It is a real struggle to be polite at times.

We had just finished looking through the entire museum when it closed at five o'clock. Mrs. Rollins led us to her car, which was nearby. On the way she warned Midge and me not to mention anything about the woman who had tried to steal the sampler. We dropped off Heloise at Mrs. Martin's house first and then headed toward Grover's Corner.

"We have decided to say nothing about what happened this afternoon," Mrs. Rollins said. "That woman is not well. By the time the policeman got her home, she was having hysterics. He went inside with her and she gave him five or six things she had stolen from the museum. We got in touch with her daughter and son-in-law, who were very upset by it all. Apparently it has happened before. They are going to make certain she goes to see a doctor about it. Since the museum got all its property back, it was decided to quietly forget about the entire matter. I doubt if she will come back after the fright you gave her, Midge. She still insists that a voice from the past spoke to her. It would be very helpful if you two would say nothing about it, except to your parents, of course."

We agreed, but I think it is a shame that Midge can't be awarded a medal or something. She deserves it, and it would be great for our think tank to say we had solved a mysterious crime. Maybe we ought to become a detective agency too.

Sunday, September 1

*I am not really writing this on Sunday. It is actually Tues-*day. So much has happened the past two days I haven't been able to keep up with my journal. But since so much happened I am making a separate entry for each day.

Mrs. Glass drove us over to Mrs. Martin's house shortly after lunch on Sunday. Mrs. Martin had already gone off to Morristown to judge a dog show. Heloise came out as soon as we drove in the driveway and actually seemed glad to see us. By two-thirty or so we were in New Hope.

New Hope is a very interesting town. A barge canal runs right through the center of it, because a long time ago mules used to haul barges up and down the Delaware River. There are lots of interesting shops, but the most interesting thing about New Hope is the tourists. Midge takes pictures of unusual jogging costumes like Rodney's, but she could really have a great collection if she took pictures of summer tourists' costumes. New Hope has some shops with weird clothes, but nothing as weird as those worn by the shoppers. Even Heloise was amazed, although she tried not to show it. After we had looked in shops for a while I persuaded Midge and Heloise to walk across the river to Lambertville. The Delaware is a beautiful river. Just below the bridge there are a lot of big rocks in the water. The river is quite shallow at this spot and there are white-water rapids. I could see that floating down the river in an inner tube was going to be interesting, especially if Heloise tried to keep that bored look on her face.

Heloise and Midge started looking through the shops in Lambertville, but then I had a stroke of luck. Heloise began to get a blister on her heel, so we went back to New Hope and sat for a while at a little sidewalk cafe. Then it was time to go meet our taxi to the Old Mill Pond Inn. The menu had lots of things on it I liked. We ordered and while we were waiting Midge looked around the big dining room. She saw something behind me that made her sit straight up in surprise. Then she began to grin.

"Henry, our one big failure may not be one at all. Look who is having dinner over there by the window."

I turned around to look. There sitting at the table by themselves were Mrs. Shultz and a dark-haired man. I wasn't certain about him at first because he looked different with a suit and tie.

"That's Don, isn't it?" Midge asked.

"It is," I agreed. "I didn't recognize him without his bulldozer."

"If you went up to look at the stage and then went out that door as though you were going to the rest room you would go fairly near their table."

"I think I'll do that," I said. I knew exactly what she meant.

I wandered out toward the lobby. Mrs. Shultz and her escort were very busy talking to each other and didn't notice as I went by. Their waiter arrived just as I passed. I watched him serve them and then went on.

"What were they eating?" Midge asked when I returned to the table.

"It wasn't buckwheat groats," I said. "He had a great big slab of rare roast beef and she had a duck."

"Hmmm," Midge said. "They look quite interested in each other. Now, if he takes her out to dinner, I suppose she is polite and invites him to her house for a meal. Then I wonder what they eat?"

"What are you two talking about?" Heloise wanted to know. "Why are you so interested in what someone else eats?"

"It just happens that the woman we are talking about is a health-food fanatic," Midge said. "Her children are growing up undernourished on a diet of yogurt and wheat germ and bean sprouts."

"Underprivileged, too," I said. "Eating what they have to eat."

"And now she is out with a new boyfriend and he's eating rare roast beef. We're hoping it's a good sign."

"No doubt about it. If she invites him over for dinner,

146

she'll have what he likes whether it's part of her diet or not," Heloise said as though she was some sort of an authority. It was the most sensible remark she'd made since we met her.

"I think we'd better call the twins in the morning," Midge said thoughtfully. "We can say we hope our long-range plan is beginning to work and ask how things are going."

"I don't see how we can claim credit for this," I said.

"We certainly can," Midge said. "They would probably have never gotten to know each other if it hadn't been for us. Not many people have such an exciting introduction either."

"What was exciting about their introduction?" Heloise asked. I suspect the one thing that doesn't bore Heloise is romance.

"Mrs. Shultz fell flat on her face in a mud puddle," I said. "And he picked her up. She was so mad she ordered him off her property."

"Why?" Heloise asked. "He's very handsome."

"It's sort of complicated," I said. "She was chasing his dog and my dog out of her flower garden and she tripped over one of them and fell in the mud."

Just then the waiter arrived with our dinners, and she didn't ask any more questions. I didn't feel like explaining it all. Also, I had come across our extra spiders when I was getting dressed and I had stuck one in my pocket just in case. It seemed a waste of money not to use them and I figured if Heloise was too bored with the evening, I might liven things up a bit with a spider.

We were only half finished with our dinner when the

show started. They turned the lights down low but you could still see to eat and that is what most people did, including me.

It was a great show. The villain was dressed in a black-and-white checkered suit and had a big handlebar mustache that he twirled every few minutes. The poor heroine's father had died, her mother was an invalid, and the villain was trying to steal her farm. There were all sorts of exciting adventures and the hero rescued the heroine just in the nick of time about six different times. The audience hissed, booed, clapped, cheered, and stomped their feet. It was a lot of fun and really exciting. I was on the edge of my chair a number of times and so was Midge.

"Well, how did you like it?" Midge asked when it was over and they turned up their lights.

"Quite amusing," Heloise said. "Of course the cast was sort of amateurish but all in all it was not bad."

I could see Midge was annoyed. While we had not spent our own money on the dinner and show, we had gone to quite a bit of trouble arranging everything. It wouldn't have hurt Heloise to act as though she had enjoyed it. I moved my feet back because if Midge accidentally kicked someone under the table, I didn't want it to be me.

Maybe they were short a waiter or two or maybe they weren't too well organized, but about half the people had been served their dessert and coffee during intermission and half had not. Lots of people were paying their checks and leaving while others, like us, had just ordered dessert. We didn't care, because the show had finished early and we had plenty of time before Midge's parents were expected.

"That blister on my heel hurts," Heloise said. "I think I'll go ask that woman outside at the desk if she has a Band-Aid. Order me a cup of coffee, will you, when our dessert comes?"

At lunch in Hopewell, Heloise had ordered coffee and put at least three heaping teaspoonfuls of sugar in it. I figured she would again, so I put my hand in my pocket and got my spider. I reached over, lifted the lid to the sugar bowl, and dropped it in. Against the white sugar the spider looked great.

"Fancy meeting you two here," a pleasant voice said.

We looked up and there were Mrs. Shultz and Don the bulldozer operator. Mrs. Schultz looked very pretty, Don looked very handsome, and they both looked very pleased with each other. I got to my feet politely and said hello. Neither Midge nor I knew quite what to say or what to do. The last time I'd seen Mrs. Shultz she had been boiling mad. I guess Don saw that I looked uneasy.

"Don't act so scared," Don said grinning. "She's not mad at either of us anymore—just our dogs."

"I'm not mad at them either," Mrs. Shultz said, laughing. "After all, if it hadn't been for all that to-do, I wouldn't have gotten to know Don. Besides, it was all an accident."

Just then a waiter came over, reached a long arm across the table, and picked up our sugar bowl. "Mind if I borrow your sugar?" he asked. "Table over here seems to be short."

"Go ahead," Midge said before I could open my mouth.

I didn't know what to do. I couldn't run after him and tell him there was a spider in the sugar, especially with Mrs. Shultz standing right there. If she believed that all the mess at her house had been an accident I certainly didn't want to do anything to change her mind.

"I do hope I didn't sound so fierce that you won't come back and see the twins," Mrs. Shultz said.

"No, we were just saying that we ought to get in touch with them," Midge said sweetly.

"You two aren't here by yourselves, are you?" Mrs. Shultz asked.

"No, we have a friend with us," Midge said. "And my mother and father will be here in a few minutes."

I frowned at her and shook my head. She was being too friendly. In another minute she might ask them to stay and meet her parents. I was having a very tough time, trying to be polite and pay attention to what Mrs. Shultz was saying and still keep my eye on that sugar bowl. The waiter had plopped it down at a big round table two tables away. There were about eight people there, including one rather large, dignified-looking woman, who apparently had asked for the sugar. At least the waiter had put it directly in front of her, and she was sitting with a cup of coffee at her place and a spoon poised in the air. Whatever she was saying seemed much more important than her coffee, because there she sat for several minutes, her spoon at the ready. She reminded me of Uncle Al, who sometimes gets arguing with something on his fork at mealtime.

"I suppose we should be getting on," Mrs. Shultz said. "Nice seeing you both."

150

"Say hello to the twins," Midge said.

They began to thread their way to the door. Midge turned to me. "What was that frown about?"

"I didn't want you to hold them up. There was a spider in that sugar you let the waiter have. If Mrs. Shultz had seen it we would be in the soup again."

"Spider in the sugar?" Midge said dumbly. It took her only a second to catch on. "You put one of our spiders in the sugar bowl? For Heloise to find?"

I nodded. The woman stretched out and was about to take the top off the sugar bowl. Then she paused again.

"Where is it?" she asked.

"Over there," I said nodding my head. "The big round table, and that big bossy-looking woman is about to put sugar in her coffee except she is too busy talking. Do you suppose I could grab a sugar bowl from some other table and quickly get over there and exchange them?"

People were starting to leave in our part of the dining room and there were several empty tables not too far away where I could grab a sugar bowl. I got to my feet.

"How are you going to explain why you want to trade?" Midge asked. "Besides, why do it? This might be more fun than the play."

"I would just as soon not find out," I said.

I started toward a nearby empty table. I'd had a pretty good idea. When I exchanged the sugar bowls I would say something about the waiter asking me to do it because that one was about empty. Actually, it hadn't been very full when I dropped the spider in it. I don't think they would have paid any attention, they were all so busy laughing and talking. I never found out. I was still on my way to get the substitute sugar bowl when the woman finally lifted the lid of her sugar bowl. Her spoon started in and then she let out a scream. It was really more a bellow than a scream. She didn't like spiders any more than Mrs. Shultz. She swept her right arm around and the sugar bowl went sailing through the air, with sugar flying everywhere. It landed almost at my feet, breaking into three pieces. Everyone still in the dining room looked around. Waiters started dashing toward the table from every direction. I think I was the calmest person there. I leaned over and picked up the pieces one at time and put them on the nearest table. As I picked up the third piece I found what I wanted. I put it in my pocket.

"What happened?" a waiter asked, rushing up and looking at the pieces of sugar bowl.

"I think someone at that table is throwing china," I said. "I almost got hit."

I went back to our table and sat down. The woman who had almost put the spider in her coffee was making a big fuss to the head waiter, who had hurried over.

"I got it," I said to Midge.

"And I got us another bowl of sugar," Midge said. "Just in case. We've had sugar all the time."

"What a yowl she made," I said. "Is everyone around here scared to death of spiders?"

"I'm not," Midge said. "There are some really cute ones out in our garden shed. But I wouldn't be surprised if Heloise was. She's just the type."

"We aren't going to find out," I said. "Once is enough."

152

By the time Heloise got back a minute or so later, everything had quieted down. Her coffee had arrived and she put three big spoons full of sugar in it. The dining room began to empty out.

"I can see why they have a stage show with dinner," Heloise said, looking around the dining room as though she didn't like anything she saw. "This place would be rather boring otherwise."

"I think it's pretty exciting at times," Midge said. "Don't you, Henry?"

I didn't answer because I was busy paying the bill and trying to figure out the tip.

We saw Midge's parents out in the lobby and got up to join them.

"Tomorrow is the day," Midge said in a low voice to me as we followed Heloise out of the dining room. "Tomorrow is our turn."

Monday, September 2

Today has been a great day. We finished our three-day job of entertaining Heloise and it turned out better than I expected. She may have almost drowned today, but at least she wasn't bored. And I certainly wasn't bored; I had a wonderful day. I'm a little sunburned on my knees, but not too badly.

Tubing on the Delaware is great sport. I suppose most people who live in eastern Pennsylvania and western New Jersey have been tubing on the Delaware. It seemed to me most of them were doing it today. There was a flotilla of people floating down the river.

You don't need much equipment to go tubing—just an inner tube. You blow it up, get in it, and float down the river. There were big truck tubes with big fat people in them, medium-sized tubes with average people in them, and little tubes with little kids in them. I don't know where all the tubes came from, since most cars have tubeless tires today. The best-size tube is one where you can put your arms over one part and your knees over the opposite side and be comfortable.

Midge furnished the tubes for us. She is an old hand at tubing on the Delaware and so we were well equipped. Mr. Glass has gone down with Midge before but this year he had a pulled tendon in one leg and didn't go along. He and Mrs. Glass drove us to just above Point Pleasant, where we started, and picked us up at Lambertville where we ended about five hours later. Of course we weren't floating all the time. We stopped for a picnic lunch.

There was a tube each for Midge, Heloise, and me. Some people had extra tubes with what I thought was a very clever arrangement. They made a sort of net and put a picnic cooler in it. I pointed out several of these to Midge.

"Looks good, but it isn't," Midge said. "Dad and I tried it one year. He even tied the cooler in place so it couldn't be dumped. It turned upside down and our entire lunch was soaked. We worked out a much better arrangement after that."

I was about to ask her what, but something came up and I didn't learn until later.

We were wearing bathing suits and we left our clothes in the car. We waded out until the water got reasonably deep, waved goodbye to Mr. and Mrs. Glass, and floated away.

You can paddle with your hands and keep your head pointed upstream if you want or you can just let the tube twirl around while you look up at the sky or at the trees along the banks, and relax. Some places the river runs quite fast, while in others it moves along slowly and quietly. You can almost go to sleep if you want, it is so peaceful. The history books have lots about how George Washington and his army crossed the Delaware in small boats during the American Revolution and then went on to defeat the Hessians in Trenton. If there had been any tubes in those days he would probably have floated down the river to Trenton. Of course, he wouldn't have done it at Christmas because it wouldn't be very comfortable floating down an icy river in a tube.

I doubt if Heloise has done a great deal of swimming. While she knows how to swim, she doesn't seem comfortable in the water. She was very nervous when we started out. Maybe she thought the Delaware is a much deeper river than most of it is. Or maybe she thought there were man-eating fish in the water, or snakes. Heloise didn't exactly say that floating down the river in an inner tube bored her, but she half pretended that it did. Now that we have gotten to know her better, Midge and I have decided she has a standard act.

"She pretends she has done everything at least twice and is tired of it all," Midge claims.

We entered the river at a great spot. We floated past several large islands and dozens of smaller islands. The river wound in and out among them. I know how Tom Sawyer and Huck Finn must have felt floating down the

Mississippi on their raft and hiding on deserted islands. Midge and I would get excited about different things and point them out to each other. Heloise pretended nothing interested her and trailed her hand in the water and looked bored. But she was enjoying herself.

We met a number of people. You wouldn't think floating down the river in an inner tube would be a good place to meet people, but it is. Sometimes, though, things got sort of interrupted. I met one boy from over near the seashore whose father manufactured parachutes. This boy, who is about my age, had taken a parachute jump. He was telling me all about it when his tube got caught on a snag in the river and I left him behind.

Partway down we bumped into a boy named Jack Simmons. He is quite a lot older than we are, and maybe he was more interested in Heloise than in us, but we all got along very well. When I say bumped into him that is exactly what I mean. We drifted down one side of an island and he went down the other. There was an eddy where the two streams met and it ended up with Midge's feet in Jack's face.

Jack goes to college at Rider College near Lawrenceville. He had a date with some girl to float down the river and she was supposed to meet him at Point Pleasant. He had left his car in Lambertville and begged a ride with someone up to Point Pleasant. When he got there she had left a message at the inner-tube place that she couldn't come. He had bought a fancy lunch for both of them and his car was way downstream. There wasn't much he could do but float down the river by himself.

Jack had his lunch in a heavy plastic bag. He had carefully sealed it with tape, leaving a big air bubble inside. It floated beside his tube, tied with a short piece of heavy cord.

We floated past Marshall Island, Treasure Island, and Prahls Island. About a mile or so below Prahls Island there is the remains of an old bridge sticking out from both sides of the river. Midge called to us and we followed her over to a quiet pool below the bridge abutment. Jack Simmons came along.

"About a mile below here is the Lumberville Wing dam," she said. "It has two wings coming out from the two sides almost to the center of the river. In the center is an open chute. When the river is low very little water goes over the two wings; practically all of it goes through the chute. But today the river is high and water will be going over the wings and really pouring down the chute. It is rough going through the chute and you may get ducked at the bottom, but it's safe. It is never safe to go over either of the two wings. It is quite a drop and you can land on rocks at the bottom. You don't *have* to go through the chute. You can get out well above the dam and walk around to the bottom. That's what I did the first time. But it's lots of fun racing down the chute. Now, if you are going down the chute, stay in the center of the river! I will go first, so if you stay behind me you will be all right. Now, who wants to shoot the chute and who wants to walk?"

"Shoot the chute," I said. If Midge was going down, I wasn't going to act scared, even if I was.

Heloise was doubtful. "Are you going down the chute?" she asked Jack Simmons.

"Of course," he said. He acted as though he was unconcerned about the whole thing, but I noticed he listened very carefully while Midge told us some more details about the dam.

We got back in the water and began floating downstream again. Jack Simmons and Heloise either didn't start out quite as soon as Midge and I or they hit a slower part of the current, because we got some distance ahead of them. I was floating along peacefully looking up at the houses along the banks when I heard a dull roar.

"Is that the water going over the dam?" I asked.

"It must be," Midge said. "I never heard it that loud before or this far away. The water must be whaling over it. Let's move a bit to the right."

The noise didn't seem to grow any louder, or else I just got used to it. The current did begin to flow noticeably faster, however. Midge began to paddle to keep her feet pointed downstream and be able to see where we were going, so I did too. We didn't look back for some time. Suddenly Midge swung around and sort of sat up in her tube.

"Get over to the center!" she screamed in alarm. "You are too far to the right!"

I looked back and saw what she was so excited about. Jack and Heloise must not have been paying attention, because they certainly weren't in the center. They were much too close to the New Jersey side of the river.

Heloise half sat up too and saw the dam not too far ahead. She panicked and began flailing around with her arms. She was spinning more than she was moving.

"Forget the tube! Swim!" Midge shouted. "And hurry!"

Heloise slipped out of her tube but hung onto it with one hand. Jack Simmons flopped out of his tube, swam the few feet to Heloise, and grabbed her with one arm. He began swimming toward the center of the river with a powerful sidestroke.

Neither Midge nor I saw anything else. The current began to flow really fast and we both turned to point our feet downstream.

"Here we go!" Midge shouted. She was about five feet ahead of me.

We went racing down the chute, bobbing up and down on the churning water. We ended in a huge boiling eddy at the bottom and both went under. We surfaced a few seconds later and both of us still had our tubes. We got our breath and paddled over to the left and looked back. We had no idea where Jack and Heloise were, but they had to be close.

A few seconds later they came racing down the chute on the far left edge. They had made it, but just barely, and neither of them had a tube. As soon as I saw that they were safe, I began looking for their tubes. I saw hers first. It had gone over the dam and was in much quieter water, floating slowly downstream. I went after it and by the time I reached it, I was able to wade. Midge shouted and pointed and then I saw Jack's too. I went after it and managed to grab it, although having to hold on to two tubes slows you down.

Jack's tube was fine, but his lunch wasn't. A rock or something had poked a hole in the plastic bag and water was sloshing around inside. I held up the bag and let the water drain out. The sandwiches and cake were all wrapped in waxed paper but I didn't have much hope for any of it. Holding all three tubes, I began moving toward the others.

Heloise had swallowed some water, but she recovered fast. She was coughing and trying to thank Jack at the same time. She seemed to feel he was a great hero and had saved her life. Maybe he did.

"Less than a mile downstream we pass under a narrow footbridge," Midge said. "On the left is Bulls Island. We'll go ashore there and have lunch and rest a while."

"That'll be nice," Heloise said. Then she saw Jack looking at his plastic bag of lunch. He was holding it up and the water was dripping out of it. "I'm sorry. I guess I ruined it."

"You didn't ruin it," Jack said. "But I think it's kind of damp."

"We've got extra lunch," Midge said. "You can eat with us."

A few minutes later we were all ashore on Bulls Island. It is a state park with tables, trash cans, rest rooms, and telephones. People were grilling hamburgers and hot dogs and one man was cooking spare ribs over a portable charcoal grill. They really smelled great.

"I promised Mom I'd call her when I got here," Midge said. "Then we get our lunch. Somebody grab a picnic table."

I was carrying the money for the telephone call in a little pocket in my swimming trunks. It was still there, even after going head over heels at the bottom of the chute. We went over to a phone booth and Midge made her call.

"Follow me and I'll show you our secret hiding place," she said.

We went back into the woods a short distance and came to a big gnarled sycamore tree. It had a hollow about four feet from the ground. Midge reached inside and brought out a shopping bag with our lunch. We carried it back to where Jack and Heloise were waiting at a table. Midge was right. There was plenty of lunch for all of us and it was good. There were roast-beef sandwiches, ham-and-cheese sandwiches, brownies, several sizable bottles of soda, and some delicious pears.

"Where did you have all this?" Heloise asked. Heloise was never bored at mealtime.

"In a hollow tree over there," Midge said. "The first year Mom and Dad and I all floated down together. That's when we had the disaster with our lunch in the picnic cooler. Mom said once was enough and the second year she was to meet us here with our lunch. Something came up and she couldn't come, so Dad and I came here, looked around, and found a place to hide our lunch. It's lots easier than trying to hang on to it all the way down."

"I'll say," Jack Simmons said, taking another sandwich. "You know, I paid about six dollars for that lunch. I threw it all over there in that trash basket. Even the lid of the cole slaw came off. Cole slaw was all over everything. Not that a little cole slaw on a water-soaked piece of chocolate cake makes any difference."

We waited a while after lunch to digest our food and

then went back into the river. It's about six miles from Bulls Island to Lambertville and the water was moving fairly fast. While there are several rapids near Stockton that are sort of fun there was nothing as exciting as the wing dam. We arrived in Lambertville about three-thirty, which was when we had planned. Mr. and Mrs. Glass were waiting for us with towels. We got semidry at least and then, sitting on our towels, drove off. Mr. Glass drove Jack Simmons to where he had left his car.

"Nice young man," Mrs. Glass said as we headed back toward Grover's Corner. "Where did you meet him?"

"Upstream a ways," Midge said. "Near some mud-bank."

"He's very brave," Heloise said. "He saved my life. Don't you think he's handsome, Mrs. Glass?"

"Very nice-looking," Mrs. Glass said cautiously. "Where is he from?"

Jack Simmons had a turned-up nose, a big wide mouth, a chin that stuck out, and freckles everywhere. I wouldn't have called him handsome, but you can never tell what girls think is handsome.

"He's from out near Pittsburgh," Heloise said. "He's going to Rider College. He's taking a liberal-arts course but he may shift to music. He and three friends have formed an orchestra. They have already played at two receptions."

"An orchestra!" Midge said. "Why didn't you tell us before? Did you get his address or telephone number?"

"Both," Heloise said. "Why?"

"Maybe we can get him to come play at our kite-flying

contest," Midge said. "You ought to come to our great kite-flying contest, Heloise. It's going to be wonderful: the air filled with kites, a beautiful big hot-air balloon up above everything for the contest judge, news reporters and photographers, lots of people cheering, speeches, and an orchestra if we find one."

Our contest is getting bigger every day.

Thursday, September 5

This week has been very quiet. Midge has gone back to school, Uncle Al is working during the day, and Agony has had a sore foot and slept most of the time. I've spent most of my time working on our kite-flying contest. I made a finished copy of my poster, Mrs. Glass drew in the kids flying kites, and we went in to a fast-print place in Princeton and had fifty copies made.

Midge took a number of the posters to school with her yesterday. She put them up on every bulletin board she could find. One boy took several to his woodworking class. The instructor said he would approve kite-making as a project. We now have eleven entrants in our contest.

We had a conference after Midge got home from school yesterday. We are sort of winding up the affairs of our think tank. We have only one active case left and that is Rodney's. We hope that will be solved by our great kite-flying contest. Of course we aren't sure about what has happened in the Shultz case, but there isn't much that we can do about it one way or another.

"I'll get Deirdre to ask a few questions," Midge said. "I'll see her at school tomorrow. We can't send them a bill, even for the spiders, unless we know whether they're still eating health food or not. But we ought to make out bills for Mrs. Martin and Mrs. Walcott and send them off or you'll be gone before we get our money."

One of the troubles about a business like a think tank is that it is hard to know what to charge. If you are a baby-sitter and all the other baby-sitters are charging a dollar an hour, for example, then you know about what you should charge. There doesn't seem to be any standard rate for thinking. We finally decided to charge Mrs. Walcott fifteen dollars for the Canada geese case and Mrs. Martin twenty dollars for entertaining Heloise. Deirdre had already paid us ten dollars for the work we did on her allowance. That was only a part payment, but since she has become a limited partner, we decided not to charge her any more.

Midge sat down and made out the two bills. They looked very neat and impressive on our letterheads. While she was doing that I began to add up what we had in the treasury.

"With eleven entries, and if we collect on both those bills, we will cover all our expenses, including the fifty-dollar first prize, and have quite a bit left over. We ought to think a little about how we are going to divide it. Deirdre has done a lot of work on this kite-flying contest."

"Hmmm, that's so," Midge admitted. "But if we are going to have extra money maybe first we ought to think about a band."

Midge is still talking about a band. Of course we don't have that much extra money and don't know where to find a band anyhow.

It was a lucky thing we made out the bills. I hadn't mailed them yet when Mrs. Martin dropped by this morning. I wish Midge could have been here. We really have a satisfied customer.

"You and your partner did a spectacular job of entertaining my granddaughter," Mrs. Martin said. "She said she never had such a wonderful visit. I was a bit doubtful about that business of floating down the Delaware, but she loved it. She's a great booster for you two. The odd part about it is that she even gives me some of the credit for her good time. Now, what do I owe you?"

"Well, Midge made out a bill," I said, handing it to her.

"That's quite businesslike," she said after looking at it for a minute. "But you aren't charging enough."

"You paid for our lunch one day, for the dinner theater, for a taxi, and for some miscellaneous things like Cokes and ice-cream cones," I explained. "And we still have eight dollars of your expense money."

"Keep it. And here is thirty dollars instead of twenty. You did a great job and ten dollars apiece a day is not a bit too much."

I thanked Mrs. Martin and decided not to mention the extra ten dollars to Midge for a few days or she would push even more for an orchestra. I did tell Uncle Al that we were going to show a healthy profit for the summer. He said that was very unusual.

"Most businesses operate at a loss their first year or even two," he said. "I hope your profit isn't so big that you have tax problems."

Saturday, September 7

We got a note from Mrs. Walcott this morning with a check for fifteen dollars. She wrote us a very nice letter saying that she was delighted with their new swans and that they were beginning to act possessive about the pond already. Also, we are now up to fourteen entrants. I told Midge about the extra ten dollars that Mrs. Martin gave us and we were sitting in our office feeling good about everything when Deirdre showed up with some bad news.

There is a boy named Radford Bradford in Midge's school who has entered the contest. He has an uncle, Theobald Bradford, who is a famous aeronautical engineer. It seems he has designed all sorts of airplane wings, tail fins, and other parts for airplanes. Radford Bradford has been boasting that he is certain to win the contest

169

because his uncle is helping him design and build his kite.

"We will simply have to disqualify him," Midge said. "And I'll enjoy telling him. Henry's rules say that if any adult helps a contestant, that contestant will be disqualified."

"But if we accuse him, he'll deny it," Deirdre said. "Did we accept his five dollars?"

"We have his five dollars and that is the only good thing you can say about Radford Bradford," Midge said. "He is mean, untrustworthy, deceitful, dishonest, and has oily hair. Let's give back his five dollars and disqualify him."

"I think Deirdre is right," I said. "Unless we can prove that his uncle is helping him, we can't disqualify him. We've had several good articles in the paper about our contest. He'd probably complain that we were being unfair and get that in the paper."

"Mary Fusoni's brother heard Radford Bradford say his uncle was helping him. Mary told Isabelle, and Isabelle told Deirdre. What more proof do you want?" Midge demanded.

We talked it over with Uncle Al and with Mrs. Glass and they both said the same thing—that it was sneaky of Radford Bradford to get his uncle to help him but that we should have proof before we disqualified him.

"I was so upset about Radford Bradford that I forgot to tell you the good news," Deirdre said. She had removed her gum for the conference. "I talked to the twins. Are they happy! Don has been over to their house twice for dinner and they had roast beef once and ham the other time. And regular human desserts. Don took the twins out to lunch twice while Mrs. Shultz was at work. He bought them hamburgers, French fries, and milk shakes and she didn't say a word when she heard about it. They think their mother and Don may get married."

"Another case solved," Midge said happily. "But do they think we solved it?"

"I'm not sure and neither are they," Deirdre said. "But I did sort of mention a bill and they expect to get one. I'd get it in fast, though, because they are on a hamburger-buying spree and they may not have any of their savings left soon."

We talked it over and finally decided to charge them ten dollars. It wasn't very much, because the spiders had cost us $3.75. Midge made out the bill and Deirdre said she would deliver it on her way home. Then we all went out in the field and drove stakes where each person holding a kite for launching was to stand. The positions have to be reasonably far apart or the strings will get tangled. On the day of the contest each stake will be numbered and the contestants will draw numbers out of a hat for position. Mr. Baines is going to bring a flatbed farm wagon to the field to use for announcements and speeches.

Sunday, September 8

It rained most of the day today. I went with Aunt Mabel and Uncle Al to visit some friends in Cranbury, New Jersey. We stayed for Sunday dinner and didn't get home until late afternoon. The rain had stopped, so I walked down to the barn with Agony. Midge appeared a few minutes later.

"We've now got seventeen entrants," she said happily. "Three people called me this morning. And guess who else I talked to on the phone?"

She had such a pleased look that I thought I knew.

"Radford Bradford, and he's sprained an ankle and has to withdraw from the contest."

"Not even near. Heloise. She's coming down for our

contest. She's been talking to Jack Simmons and his group might, just might, come play."

"How much?" I asked.

"We haven't got that far yet," Midge said. "Heloise will let me know."

Wednesday, September 11

We now have nineteen contestants. Even the weather report looks good for the great kite-flying contest. We have had some more disturbing news about Radford Bradford though. One boy saw his kite and said it was the slickest, best-looking kite he'd ever seen. Radford Bradford has flown it twice, according to reports, and is strutting around school saying no one else has a chance.

I talked to Rodney today. His kite is all ready, except for some decorating he wants to do. He has heard about Radford Bradford's kite too and is worried.

"My kite is the best one I ever made," he said. "I sure hope it beats Radford Bradford's. My dad is all excited about the contest and he and my mother and my sister are all coming."

For a while today we thought we had a way to disqualify Radford Bradford and his fancy kite. Someone told Midge he was over sixteen, but it wasn't so. His birthday is three days after the contest. Midge wanted to postpone the contest for a week but I will be gone by then. Also, we have announced the contest and really can't postpone it unless it is very stormy both Saturday and Sunday.

The Shultz twins paid their bill today. They gave the money to Deirdre at school and she gave it to Midge. With the nineteen entries and the other money we have collected we have almost a hundred and fifty dollars after expenses. Deducting the fifty-dollar prize we will still have a hundred. I tried to get Midge to discuss how we would divide it. It is complicated, what with Deirdre being just a limited partner. She had nothing to do with the Canada geese case or with Heloise but she has done a lot for the kite-flying contest.

"We'll have time to decide that later," Midge said. "I have a slew of homework. My teachers don't make any allowance for the time I have to spend on our contest."

Sunday, September 15

The great kite-flying contest is over. We have closed our Think Tank for the year and I have spent a good part of the day packing to go to Manila. In a few days I'll be back in school. It seems they found replacements for the two missing teachers. I was too tired to write in my journal last night, so I am doing it now.

Friday night Midge got a call from Heloise. She had arranged for Jack Simmons and his band to play from two-thirty on. She wasn't certain exactly how much it was going to cost but she said it would be much less than their usual rate.

It was a great day. The weather was perfect, although Midge and I weren't sure whether we were happy about that or not, since it meant there was no way to disqualify

Radford Bradford. Everything went according to schedule. The orchestra arrived on time, the balloon arrived on time, and Mr. Baines brought the flatbed farm wagon on time. There was a big crowd in the field by three o'clock. People came from everywhere. There were several photographers. One was from the newspaper and the other may have been from a magazine. Deirdre thought so but we don't know.

Getting the balloon inflated and up in the air was quite a complicated operation, but it was up with Mr. Baines and Mr. Matuska in it by the time everything began at three. Midge and I got up on the wagon and first I announced the rules of the contest and what the prize would be. Then Midge introduced Mr. Baines. He couldn't really hear anything she said up in that noisy balloon, but she had arranged signals with him and he waved to everyone when he was introduced.

Deirdre held the hat and announced the different positions as the contestants drew their numbers from an old hat belonging to Uncle Al. Agony ran around and barked happily at everything. We had planned to have Deirdre shoot off the cap pistol to start the contest but she had to hold a kite. Several contestants had asked us to have someone hold their kites, which had been easy enough to arrange when we knew a couple of days ahead of time. Radford Bradford appeared about three minutes before everything was to begin and asked for an assistant. There was no one left to do it but Deirdre.

"He probably hasn't any friends," Midge said. "It would serve him right if Deirdre poked a finger through his kite."

I don't know much about music. It seemed to me that the orchestra was louder than it was good, but the crowd seemed to enjoy it. Heloise certainly did. She stood right beside it the whole time and didn't wear any ear plugs either. It played for half an hour and then took a five-minute intermission when everything began. All the kites were lined up, and everything seemed set to go, when Radford Bradford objected that Deirdre wasn't holding his kite high enough. Of course that was silly because the contest wasn't to be decided until the kites had been in the air for twenty minutes. Midge was right about Radford Bradford. He is a pain in the neck and he does have oily hair. Anyhow, to keep him from complaining we found a box for Deirdre to stand on. Finally Midge fired the pistol.

All the kites but one got airborne. Two more didn't fly very high before they went into a spin and then a nosedive. The remaining sixteen all went up very nicely. The breeze was just right. Some of the kites were beautiful. There were kites with colored stripes, kites with stars, kites with initials, kites decorated with faces, and kites that looked like dragons. I have to admit that Radford Bradford's kite was the most impressive one of all. It was covered with a silver-colored plastic with a big gold star in the center. Rodney's kite, which was only four positions away, looked ugly by comparison. He had decorated it with big splotches of red and green and purple. Midge says Rodney is going to be a famous modern artist someday.

Rodney's kite may not have been very pretty, but it could fly. After the first few minutes anyone could see that the contest was really between Rodney and Radford

Bradford. Their kites kept going up and up and finally Mr. Matuska had to signal to his assistant to let out more rope on the tether.

. No one on the ground could tell who was the winner. Heloise kept the time, and when the twenty minutes was up, Jack Simmons blew a long note on his trumpet. Mr. Matuska and Mr. Baines waved that they had heard and the balloon began to come down. They didn't let it collapse, as Mr. Matuska planned to fly away. He stayed in it, but Mr. Baines climbed out when the basket finally touched the ground. He wouldn't say anything to anyone, including Midge, until he had climbed up on the wagon. I thought Midge was going to blow up with excitement. I would like to have known myself, but Mr. Baines wouldn't talk. He was having a great time and had really enjoyed being up in the balloon. I don't think his wife did though. I think she held her breath the whole time he was up.

"It was a very close contest," he announced finally. "Two kites, and I think you all could see which two, were very close. But I award the prize to the multicolored kite. It went a tiny bit higher and also it was better balanced. The silver kite with the big gold star tilted slightly to its right."

The crowd cheered and the band began to play. Midge jumped up and down screaming something and Agony barked. Rodney climbed up on the wagon and Midge and I congratulated him and gave him his fifty dollars. No one could hear what we said because the band was playing so loudly. Everybody could see us give him the money, though.

"Speech!" someone shouted. "Speech from the winner."

We looked around for Rodney, but he had disappeared. A minute later Deirdre came over to the wagon and shouted something which I couldn't understand. I don't know whether it was the band or her gum that interfered.

"What did you say?" Midge shouted and pointed to her cheek.

The band stopped playing and Deirdre took her gum out at the same time. "Hurry up, the balloon's waiting," she said.

"What?"

"The balloon is waiting. We're all going up. Come on!"

Rodney's father had rented the balloon to celebrate Rodney's winning the contest, and Rodney was taking us all with him. Usually the balloon carries only four adults, but since Midge and Deirdre were so small Mr. Matuska said we could all go. With him we were five. There wasn't much extra room but we squeezed in.

I was the last one to climb in. Mr. Matuska cast off the tether rope and we began to rise. It was great. The band began to play. Uncle Al, Aunt Mabel, Mr. and Mrs. Glass, Heloise, Rodney's family, the Shultz twins, Mrs. Shultz, Don the bulldozer operator, and almost everyone in Grover's Corner waved and cheered as we floated upward. Agony ran around in circles and barked. The balloon kept going higher and higher, until soon we were floating above the trees. You could still hear the orchestra.

"That orchestra is really loud," I said to Midge. "Did you ever find out how much they charge?"

"I did," Midge said. "I've already paid them. They were expensive, but they were worth it. And we still show a profit."

"How much?" I asked. I was suspicious. She acted too unconcerned.

"Well, after paying for the copying work and everything and the orchestra we have a net profit left of two dollars and twenty cents."

"That's not much," I said. I was sort of stunned.

"It solves a lot of things," Midge said. "Dividing up the money won't be much of a problem, and we won't have to worry about taxes."

Deirdre started to say something and coughed. Then she let out a wail. "I lost my gum!"

I looked over the side. "It didn't fall on anybody."

"Just as well you lost it," Midge said. "Gum solidifies at high altitudes and is ruined."

"No, it doesn't," Deirdre said. "It was up once before today and it was all right."

"What do you mean?" I asked.

"When Radford Bradford and I were shouting back and forth about holding his kite higher, he couldn't understand what I was saying. So I took my gum out. There was no place else to put it so I parked it on one of the sticks of his kite. Before I could get it back, Midge fired the pistol. I was worried the whole time it was up, so when the contest ended I went out and caught his kite for him. There it was, safe and sound."

"Which side of the kite?" I asked. "Right or left?"

"Right."

Midge and I both looked around. Rodney was busy talking to Mr. Matuska.

"I move we take what's left of the treasury and buy Deirdre some new gum," I said.

"I vote for that," Midge agreed.

The few people we could see were so far away that they looked like ants. The orchestra had packed up its instruments and had gone. The big day was over and our Think Tank was out of business. But as Midge said later, "What a way to go out of business!"

SHOP AT HOME FOR QUALITY CHILDREN'S BOOKS AND SAVE MONEY, TOO.

Now you can have Dell's Readers Service Listing filled with hundreds of titles including many fine children's books. Plus, take advantage of our unique and exciting bonus book offer which gives you the opportunity to purchase a Dell book for only 50¢.
Here's how!

Just order any five books at the regular price. Then choose any other single book listed (up to a $5.95 value) for just 50¢. Use the coupon below to send for the Dell Readers Service Listing today.

DELL READERS SERVICE LISTING
P.O. Box 1045
South Holland, Illinois 60473

Ms./Mrs./Mr._____

Address _____

City/State _____ Zip_____

DFCYR–11/88